Taken by the Cat

Taken by the Cat

Highland Shifters
Book 2

Caroline S. Hilliard

CONTENTS

ABOUT THIS BOOK

He doesn't believe in love. But fate doesn't care what you believe.

Stephanie has been captured. Again. And with a broken leg her hope of escape is practically nonexistent. She is to be mated to Jack, the cruel and powerful panther alpha.

But for now, she still has her dreams and memories. Memories of a gorgeous man carrying her down from the mountain after her accident. A man she could easily see herself falling for. Her savior. And the star of her dreams, for as long as she can hold on to them.

The sight of Stephanie being dragged away by a couple of thugs, has Michael storming off the train to get to her. But before he can reach them, they take off in a grey van.

Ever since he found her up on the mountain with a broken leg, she has occupied the back of his mind. He has no idea why, though. It's not like he has feelings for her or anything. Or does he? He can't seem to forget about her and seeing her again only reinforces his need to find her. And he will find her, no matter what it takes.

This work is intended for mature audiences. It contains explicit sexual situations and violence that some readers may find disturbing.

CHAPTER 1

Stephanie watched as the alpha panther paced in agitation. He was furious with his goons for not considering her broken leg while kidnapping her. Not because he cared about her being in pain. Compassion was a trait that had clearly passed him by without making an impression.

"I can't have a mate with a limp. How would that look?" The alpha was yelling at the two burly shifters standing to the right of the door just inside his large office. "What kind of respect do you think I'll get if my woman is a cripple? You fucking idiots!"

Steph was getting some satisfaction from the way Jack was abusing his men. They hadn't exactly been gentle with her when they grabbed her in broad daylight in Fort William. She could have screamed to attract attention, but what would that have gotten her? More abuse, that was what. And involving innocent bystanders would only have led to bloodshed.

She was lying on the couch with her leg up to

reduce the swelling. All to prevent any permanent damage to her leg, and to Jack's precious reputation and status as the clan alpha.

"And you." He rounded on her, his eyes a little crazy with anger. "Why the fuck did you run in the first place? You stupid bitch, almost ruining our mating." He approached the couch and squatted next to her. The corners of his thin lips raised in a vicious smile, if the grimace could even be called a smile. "But we will mate. The ceremony is all planned. I'll fuck you in the garden for all to see, and then you'll be mine."

Disgust must have shown on her face, because his face contorted in fury. "You will take me with a smile on your face, bitch. And when I stop, you will beg me for more." His low snarly voice was far more frightening than his yelling.

Steph didn't see it coming and had no time to brace herself. His fist slammed into her stomach, causing her to double over and gasp for breath. Nausea rolled through her, and she just about threw up.

"Look what you made me do?" Jack was yelling again. A good sign really. The worst was probably over. "How are you going to be able to have my cubs if you make me hit you like that? Fuck!"

He walked over to his men again, leaving her alone. Breathing was difficult but possible, and she focused on making each shallow breath count.

Closing her eyes, Steph let her mind wander, and it went where it had so many times the last few days. Beautiful light-brown eyes staring at her with concern. Short black hair and a stunningly handsome face. Chiseled jaw and high cheekbones suggested a Scandinavian bloodline, but coloring more in line with southern Europe or Latin America. But his accent revealed that Michael was American.

She should have died up there in the hills. Finally managing to escape the panthers, she had run for days. But the fear and hunger had weakened her and made her lose focus, and when she fell and got stuck in between the boulders, she knew that was it. But her will to live made her cry for help from time to time. There had been tourists wandering around up there in the summer, and she thought perhaps someone would hear her.

Michael had found her up on that mountain, him and his friends. And he had made sure she was comfortable while they waited for someone to help her get loose from the boulder that was resting on her leg. Afterward he had carried her down from the mountain, holding her close to his hard, strong body.

The memory was so clear, but Steph knew it would fade with time. She would never forget him, though, her gorgeous rescuer. She would hold onto the memory of him for as long as she could, until she lost herself.

∞∞∞∞

Michael put his bag and jacket in the car he had rented. This was crazy; he knew that. But he couldn't forget the image of Stephanie in pain as she was being escorted by two big men through the parking lot outside the Fort William train station. By the time he had gotten off the train, they were driving away in a gray van, and all he knew was the van's license plate number and that they were heading north.

The people at the hospital had been less than helpful. There was nobody by the name of Stephanie that had been a patient there in the last few days, and when he suggested she might have given a false name, they wouldn't listen. He'd even offered them money for information about any female patients in their twenties that had been brought in last Tuesday, but that didn't go down well. Michael was told to leave before they called the police.

He knew the van had been heading north from the train station, but there were several roads they could have followed after that. They could have headed west toward Mallaig, north toward Inverness, or even followed the road to the north of Ben Nevis going east. From there the possibilities were endless.

There was really just one thing left to do.

Michael pulled out his cell phone and found the contact he wanted. It rang several times before a man answered.

"Michael." The gruff voice didn't sound happy. "It's five thirty in the morning. I was just getting ready to shag my mate before work. This had better be good."

"Chris. This is important to me, and I'll owe you one."

There was a sigh at the other end of the line. "Okay, what do you want?"

"I need you to run a license plate number for me. In Scotland. ASAP." Thank God, he had good connections. He had made sure to do people favors whenever it was within his capability. That kind of network of people indebted to him was worth its weight in gold, and it would help him the day he challenged his father for the role of alpha in their clowder. And that day would come soon. He had no doubt about it.

"In Scotland? Okay. I'll text you the details as soon as I've got them."

"Thanks." He ended the call and quickly texted Chris the license plate number.

Michael got in the car and drove to the nearest pub. He might as well eat while he waited for Chris to find the name and address of the owner of the van. After ordering, he found a table in the back of the pub.

He had just sat down when his cell phone rang. After extracting it from his pocket, he saw it was James calling him. Michael had been in Scotland for a week, with his friends James and Carlos and their wives, Ann and Marna. Jennie had been part of their group as well until recently when she had met Trevor, a wolf shifter who had turned out to be her mate. That had put a dent in Michael's plan to secure Jennie as his mate. His father had set a deadline for Michael to find a mate, or his father would pick one for him. And his time was almost up. Michael didn't really want a mate, but he would rather pick a woman himself than have his father do it for him.

"James, I'm sorry I took off without saying anything. Something came up."

"Yeah, I realized that from your text." James didn't sound pleased. "What exactly came up?"

James wasn't Michael's alpha, but he was an alpha that was also Michael's friend. Sometimes James let his alpha power come out to try to influence or push Michael, and it had always irritated him until he recently understood that it only happened whenever

James was concerned and wanted to protect his friends or family. It wasn't a power play but a sign of him caring.

Michael sighed and ran his hand through his hair in frustration. "I saw Stephanie as we were pulling into the train station. Two big brutes were hauling her across a parking lot, and they took off in a van. I'm beginning to see why she was so scared. She wasn't up in those hills for a nice walk. She was running away."

"You should've said something. We would've come with you to help." James sounded concerned and a bit angry.

"Thank you, James, but what about your wife? I know you wouldn't want to put her at risk. And anyway, there wasn't time to explain. I wanted to get to Stephanie as soon as possible, to save her from those assholes not giving a shit about her injured leg."

"So, what's your plan?"

"I have a guy running the license plate of the gray van to get the details of the owner. Perhaps an address. It's worth checking out." Michael was hopeful that it would be that easy, but even if that lead turned out to be bogus, he wasn't going to give up.

"So, what? You're going to go to this address all by yourself, knock on the door, and ask for Stephanie?" James's anger was rising. It was evident in his voice.

Michael was silent for a few seconds. It did sound stupid when put like that. He sighed. "I haven't really planned that far yet. I'll need to think of something."

"Damn right you do. What do you think will happen to you if you're caught? Not to mention what will happen to her if they think she had something to do with you turning up on their doorstep."

Michael felt his blood run cold. He was an idiot. Running into this like he was a crown prince commanding respect would be a disaster. He might have a powerful clowder behind him back home, but in Scotland, he was a nobody.

Michael took a calming breath. "As I said, I'll have to think of something. I'll give you a call when I know more."

"Yes, you will. Before you go off on your own. We'll get off at the first stop and catch the next train back to Fort William."

Michael almost accepted, but then he thought about James and Carlos joining him in his search for Stephanie. There was certainly strength in numbers, but the three of them would draw more attention to themselves than he would by himself. And he had a feeling staying under the radar was imperative.

"No, James. Don't change your plans for this. At least not yet. Let me check out a few things first. Just to get an impression of what kind of people we're dealing with. Go and enjoy Edinburgh with your wife. I'll be in touch tomorrow."

There was no response from James for several seconds.

"Do not attempt to contact them by yourself, okay? You need backup for that. Tell us what you find out, and we'll come up with a plan together." James's tone was clipped. He was clearly not happy about this, but he wasn't pushing to come back and take charge either.

"Will do. I'll call you tomorrow when I know more." That would give Michael twenty-four hours to find and rescue Stephanie discretely without dragging any more people into this.

∞∞∞∞

Steph woke up with a start. She had fallen asleep on the couch in Jack's office after receiving some painkillers. Not any normal over-the-counter medicine, apparently, judging from the effects it had on her. It had knocked her out cold. For how long she had no idea.

She opened her eyes slowly, before she glanced around the room without moving her head. Steph wanted to get an overview of her surroundings before alerting anyone to her being awake.

There wasn't anyone in the room with her, which was a surprise. She hadn't expected Jack to ever leave her by herself in a room again after her lucky escape about a week ago. But at the moment, she was all alone and thank the stars for that.

Steph sat up slowly and winced as nausea rolled through her. It was probably due to the drugs or Jack's fist, or perhaps both. Not something she hadn't experienced before.

After a couple of minutes of not moving, the nausea slowly subsided. She took a deep breath to find her equilibrium before getting to her feet. Or rather foot. One of her legs was useless, and even with the cast, she couldn't put any weight on it without crying out.

Slowly, with the help of the couch and then the wall, she inched toward the door out of Jack's office. It was the only door in the windowless room, so her options were limited. Steph had no hope of escaping a second time, but sitting around waiting for whatever was going to happen to her wasn't her style. She might still be afraid of Jack, with good reason, but after being scared for months, she was getting to a point where her fear was turning into numbness.

The door opened without a sound, and she found herself standing face to face with one of Jack's thugs. He had obviously been standing guard right outside the door.

"Bathroom." It was the only thing she could think of as an explanation for being up and about against Jack's specific orders.

The brute studied her face for a few seconds before nodding. Then, he picked her up and carried her down the corridor. They rounded a corner and emerged into a large room. She had a few seconds to scan the room before the guy carrying her turned and opened a door on the left.

They entered a small room with a toilet and a wash basin. It was old and worn but seemed reasonably clean. The brute lowered her feet to the floor and let her find her footing before letting her go. Good to know that he had learned his lesson about considering her injury. Jack's reasons for wanting her healthy were in no way honorable, but at least there were some good side effects.

Steph looked at her face in the mirror above the wash basin. Tired eyes with dark shadows under them stared back at her. Her skin was pale and drawn, giving her a sickly look. Not exactly a picture of health and vitality.

Narrowing her eyes in consideration, she studied the image of her own body in the mirror. Skinny was the word that came to mind. Almost to the point of boney. She had lost a lot of weight over the last few months. Not a surprise really, considering what she had been through, but she was still a bit shocked at the transformation.

Steph had been a fun-loving tour guide when she met Jack five months ago. Taking tourists on daytrips hiking in the mountains around Aviemore had been perfect for her, quite often ending with partying with the same tourists into the small hours. Plenty of fun and no worries. Her life had been a blast.

When she'd met Jack, she had been a bit reluctant at first. A relationship with a man was not part of her plans. She was all about short-term fun. But he had managed to charm his way through her defenses with his good looks, flowers, and obvious adoration. And when after a few weeks he wanted to show her his estate a bit north of Fort William, she had accepted on the condition that they would only stay the weekend.

Everything had changed at that point. As soon as they stepped into his house, his whole personality changed. From a charming and considerate man emerged a brute and a bully, and Steph was reduced from a revered girlfriend to one of Jack's possessions.

At first she had been angry and rebelled loudly, but all that did was provoke Jack's fury, and she soon learned to fear his fists. There was one thing that was even more disturbing than his temper, however, and that was his acting skills. She had been well and truly fooled to believe he really liked her, even thought that he might be falling in love with her. And even though Steph didn't harbor the same feelings for him, she had been feeling privileged to have caught the interest of such a nice man.

Steph sighed as she stared at herself in the mirror. How different her life would have been if she hadn't met Jack. Somehow, she could understand his interest in her five months ago. She had been relatively good-looking and popular with the opposite sex. What she didn't understand was what Jack still saw in her. He was all about appearances, showing off his superiority at every opportunity. And Steph was in no way something to show off anymore, with her gaunt figure and sickly complexion.

She went to the toilet and then washed her hands while considering her situation. Maybe she could use her current condition to her advantage by playing into Jack's superiority complex. It might not improve her situation, but it was worth a try. Anything was better than her current prospects.

Steph was just about to open the door and exit the small room, when her mind touched upon what she had seen in the large room outside. Jack was there as well as the other goon. It seemed to be only the three of them in the building, in addition to her. The room was set up like some kind of workshop with a storage area on the far side.

What had grabbed her attention, though, was the large table close to the center of the room. On it there were a lot of bags lined up, containing what looked like white powder. There was no doubt as to what it was, and Steph wasn't really surprised. Jack fit the typical image of a drug lord perfectly.

She had been in a bad situation before, but Steph suddenly realized it was even worse than she had thought. Jack wasn't just the alpha of the large panther clan in the area. He was also a powerful drug lord with connections in the criminal world.

CHAPTER 2

Michael had finally heard from Chris about the license plate number. It had taken longer than he expected, but considering what Chris had been able to find out, the extra time was worth it. Apparently, the van was a rental, but after hacking into the rental company's system, Chris had been able to find the name of the current driver. Or rather the company renting the van long-term. A holding company registered to Jack Malcolm Williams.

That was all good information but not very useful in itself to locate Stephanie. Chris hadn't stopped there, however. He had gone on to identify all the properties registered to the company or to Jack. There were several properties around Scotland, but of particular interest was a warehouse just on the outskirts of Fort William and an estate a bit farther north. Both were locations where the two assholes could have taken Stephanie.

Michael drove past the warehouse and turned right

at the next intersection. After pulling into the parking lot by a restaurant, he parked and got out of the vehicle. After a little stroll around the area and a careful crossing of two backyards, he emerged among the trees at the back of the warehouse.

The gray van was parked right next to the only door, and the two windows facing him were completely covered on the inside by what looked like dark fabric. If he was going to enter the building from the back, he would have no choice but to go in blind.

Michael spent a few minutes checking the side of the building to his right, carefully hugging the shadows along the fence to the neighboring property. There were a few small windows, but they were all covered by the same dark fabric. The opposite side of the building was set tightly up against a tall fence and wasn't accessible.

Frowning in consideration, Michael stared at the back door. By going in he could be walking directly into an ambush. There was no way of knowing who was inside or how many, and even if there were only the three of them, Stephanie and the two thugs, he might be at a disadvantage if they were shifters. Worst case, there were more people in there. Then he would be truly fucked.

On the other hand, there was no way they would be expecting him. They had no idea who he was or why he was there. And the two assholes might not be shifters at all. They could just as well be human, rendering Michael's job easy. Two humans against one shifter were never good odds for the humans, even if they were big and burly.

The image of Stephanie being abused by the two

brutes came back into his mind, and his jaw set in determination. He couldn't wait for backup. Even if he contacted James immediately, it would be hours before his friends arrived. There was no telling what could happen to Stephanie in the meantime. Several hours had already passed since Michael saw her outside the train station.

His mind set, Michael carefully made his way to the back door. Putting his ear to the door, he listened intently. Nothing. There were no sounds from inside, so he had no way of knowing where the occupants were located relative to the door.

He put his hand on the door handle and carefully pressed down. The door slowly swung inward without a sound, revealing a long corridor. Michael breathed out a silent sigh of relief and took a step into the corridor. He stopped and listened. Still nothing. He was starting to worry they weren't present. Perhaps they had just come to this place to change vehicles, leaving the gray van that could be identified. After all, they had kidnapped a woman in broad daylight.

There was carpet on the floor in the corridor, muffling his footsteps. He made his way slowly down toward the end, where the corridor made a sharp turn to the right. He might as well have a look around to see if he could find anything to help him understand why they had taken Stephanie.

Approaching the turn in the corridor, Michael carefully snuck a peek around the corner. He was not prepared for the sight that met him.

The two assholes he had seen with Stephanie earlier were sitting on a couch, both reading magazines. What grabbed his attention, though, was Stephanie's unmoving body on the floor. Michael couldn't see her face since her head was turned the other way. A man was standing next to her, staring down at her with a menacing expression on his face. Whatever he had done to her had either rendered her unconscious or dead.

Michael must have made a sound because three pairs of eyes were suddenly staring at him in astonishment. Before he could even utter a syllable to try to diffuse the situation, they were on him. Their speed was a clear indication they weren't human, and it didn't take Michael long to catch the scent of panther as the thugs pressed him up against the wall.

The third man, the one who had been standing next to Stephanie, approached at a leisurely pace. His eyes were narrow as he studied Michael's face. Michael had never seen the man before, and he would bet money that the man had never before set eyes on Michael either.

"I'm so sorry, sir." Michael gave the man his most sincere and regretful look. "I've clearly come at a bad time. You're busy and I can come back—"

"Whatever." The man cut him off, before his face twisted into a sneer. "Too late now, isn't it? You've already seen too much."

"What?" Michael tried for innocent. There wasn't much else he could do at this stage. The damage was already done. "A woman sleeping on the floor? Nothing wrong with that, sir, I'm sure. We all get a bit worn out at times."

"Nice try, fucker. What do you think I am? An idiot?" The man put his face right up to Michael's and sniffed. Then he frowned and took a step back. "What are you? There's none like you around here."

Michael had to come up with an explanation fast. A shifter entering another shifter's property could be deemed an act of aggression at the best of times. "I'm a wereserval, sir, from the largest and most respected clowder in America. I'm here looking for Jack Williams. My contact told me this was one of his places of business."

The man narrowed his eyes at Michael, clearly suspicious. Several seconds went by while the man was staring at him in contemplation. Michael could get no indication from the man's expression as to his thoughts. This could go either way, and Michael was starting to regret that he hadn't at least sent James the information he had been able to get from Chris.

The man suddenly stepped up to Michael with a smile on his face and held out his hand. "I'm Jack."

Michael was a bit taken aback at the sudden change in attitude, but he quickly recovered. The two assholes released him, and Michael stretched out his right hand and gripped Jack's hand in a firm handshake. "I'm Michael Bianchi. Pleased to meet you, Jack."

A moan from the floor had them all turning toward Stephanie. She slowly turned her head, and Michael noticed that her eyes were open before they landed on him. He fought to keep a neutral expression on his face as his gaze took in the bruise on her cheek right below her left eye.

"About bloody time." Jack's voice was hard and menacing. "We need to leave. Now!" His head swung back to Michael with a smirk. "I guess you'll be coming with us."

The two thugs gripped Michael and held him

between them. The short reprieve was over as fast as it had come.

A small sound from Stephanie had Jack turning back to her, and Michael inwardly swore. He had hoped she would draw as little attention to herself as possible. It was better if Jack's attention remained on Michael. The guy obviously had no qualms about beating a woman.

Jack covered the distance to Stephanie in a few long strides and picked her up none too gently. He carried her toward them using one arm under her back and the other under her knees. All the while Stephanie was staring at Michael with a mixture of awe and horror on her face.

Michael was brought down the corridor and out the door by the two assholes. They had a firm grip on him like he might try to get away from them, but he followed without offering any resistance. It was no point. He had no doubt he would be taken down quickly if he tried anything. Perhaps even killed and disposed of.

They stopped by the back of the van, and Jack walked up to them with Stephanie in his arms.

The man on Michael's left opened the back door of the van and was about to lead Michael to the open door.

"Wait!" Jack's voice was like a bark, and the two assholes with Michael between them turned toward their boss. Jack moved to the door and put Stephanie down on the floor in the back of the van.

She whimpered, and Michael's gaze snapped to her face. He had been trying not to stare at her. He had no doubt that any attention Michael gave Stephanie would be taken out on her with some form of violence. Jack was that kind of bastard.

Michael quickly averted his eyes, but apparently not quick enough. Whether it was him looking at Stephanie or something else that provoked Jack, Michael had no idea. Pain suddenly exploded in his groin, and he lost the ability to stand and to breath.

Barely aware of what was happening, Michael landed with a thud on the floor in the back of the van. His whole world was filled with pain. Jack's fist had met with his groin before Michael had been able to move or brace for the impact, and the man hadn't been holding back. If Michael had been human that area of his body would have had serious permanent damage. He probably wouldn't have been able to function as a normal man ever again. As it was, his shifter nature would repair all the damage, but it would probably take about twenty-four hours of serious pain before he was back to his old self.

***

Steph gasped when Jack suddenly slammed his fist into Michael's groin. It was vicious behavior, even for Jack. He didn't have any problem with inflicting pain, but he usually had his goons do it for him. She had witnessed them breaking some poor sod's fingers several times as punishment for something or other, but she had never seen any of them attacking a man the way Jack did with Michael.

Michael landed beside her on the floor of the van, but Steph was too shocked to object or do anything. Jack's voice had her turning to him and seeing the sneer on his face.

"Can't have the asshole try anything with my mate.

I don't think there's any risk of that now." Jack was chuckling as the door slammed shut, locking her in the back of the van with Michael.

She held her breath as she stared at Michael's unmoving body. He was lying on his back with his legs a little apart, and he didn't make a sound. If she hadn't noticed the way his jaw was clamped shut in pain, she would have believed he was unconscious.

A wheezing sound escaped from his compressed lips, and she realized his breathing was all but nonexistent. "Michael?" She studied him for any sign he could hear her, but there was no change. "You have to breath. Please."

Steph couldn't even imagine the kind of pain he must be in. Jack was extremely strong, and the brute force he had exhibited when hitting Michael would be more than enough to break something delicate between his legs. She felt nauseated just thinking about it, and tears welled in her eyes. This just couldn't be happening. Her beautiful savior hurt. By Jack.

"Michael!" She tried for a more commanding tone without raising her voice. Steph was getting seriously worried about him. He did not seem to be breathing properly. Only a little wheezing at irregular and far too infrequent intervals. She had heard of people dying from extreme pain, but surely he wouldn't. Michael was a shifter. At least she hoped so.

Steph smoothed her hand over his forehead and said his name again and again. But another minute passed by without any change.

Closing her eyes, she made a decision. She had vowed never to do it again, but her vow wasn't worth this man's wellbeing. Perhaps even his life. Steph would do whatever she could to ease his suffering, no matter what the consequences. She placed her right hand gently against his groin and closed her eyes.

***

Michael slowly rose from the black swamp of pain he had been in, and he sucked in air like he had been diving for too long and had just come up to the surface. Heat was pulsing in his groin and spreading throughout his lower body, bringing with it a numbness to the pain. He sighed in relief and just breathed. There was no feeling quite like the absence of pain after experiencing something excruciating.

The events leading up to Jack's attack came back to him, and Michael reached out with his senses to try to establish his current situation.

He was lying on his back. The floor was moving, and he could hear the hum of a car engine, so his guess was that he was in the back of the gray van. There were no other noises that he could pick up. A warm scent of honey and grass surrounded him, and he suddenly noticed something warm pressed against his right hip and thigh. His heartrate picked up as he recognized the scent. Stephanie.

Michael slowly opened his eyes and took in the woman sitting with her legs outstretched beside him. Her eyes were closed. The bruise on her cheek was blue and swollen, but she was still as beautiful as he remembered. Her long chestnut hair was in a ponytail. A few strands had escaped and were caressing her bare shoulders. Her white tank top was streaked with dirt, but it hugged her small breasts nicely. She was skinnier than he remembered, but then she had been wearing a thick sweater when he carried her down from the mountain.

He let his gaze follow her right arm, which was stretched out toward him, and frowned when he saw her hand on his groin. Michael's eyes snapped back up to her face and that was when he noticed her expression of concentration. His pain was gone, and somehow she had something to do with it.

"Stephanie?" His tone was gentle, almost a whisper. She might not be aware that he had surfaced from the world of pain he had been in, and he didn't want to scare her.

"Just give me a few more minutes, Michael." She'd spoken slowly and didn't open her eyes.

He spent the time studying her face in more detail. Her complexion was pale, and she looked tired. He could see the sweat gathering at her hairline. Whatever she was doing demanded focus and strength, and he felt a bit bad for letting her carry on when she obviously needed the energy herself. But he didn't tell her to stop. This was something she was giving freely, and the pain relief she was providing him would help him prepare for whatever happened to them next.

They were on their way somewhere. Michael had no idea where. But more likely than not, it would be somewhere more remote, reducing their opportunity of getting help by attracting someone else's attention.

He let his eyes wander around the back of the van they were in. It was closed off from the cab and the only door was at the back of the vehicle. Any escape would have to be through that door, but even without his injuries he wouldn't risk jumping from the moving van with Stephanie. She seemed to be human, even though she had special abilities, and Michael would never risk her life like that. And leaving her behind while making his escape wasn't an option.

Stephanie sighed, and his eyes snapped to her face just as her eyes opened. Whatever he had thought to say vanished from his mind as he stared into her beautiful hazel eyes. Her look conveyed both worry and sadness, but there was something more there. Interest? Curiosity? He wasn't sure, but it pulled the corners of his mouth up into a smile as they kept staring at each other.

Michael hadn't noticed just how beautiful her hazel eyes were when he found her up in the hills. But then she had been in a lot of pain at the time, so that might have had something to do with it. Pain. Why had she been in so much pain if she had the ability to take it away? His pain was gone, replaced by a pulsing heat radiating from her hand down there touching him.

He frowned when he suddenly felt his cock start to lengthen and thicken in his pants. It shouldn't be possible with the extent of his injuries. He had expected at least a couple of days before regaining full function. Had Stephanie given him more than just pain relief? Did she have the ability to heal as well?

Michael's whole body jerked when need pounded through him, originating from her hand stroking his erect member through the fabric of his jeans. "Stephanie." He hissed her name as her hand slid firmly up and down his length.

"Stephanie!" he repeated, this time more firmly but without raising his voice. Grabbing her wrist gently, he lifted her right hand away from his engorged cock. Michael was tempted to let her continue stroking him to completion, but this wasn't the time or the place.

Stephanie gasped and her eyes widened. She visibly swallowed and quickly looked away from him. A deep-red blush infused her face.

Michael let go of her wrist, and she fisted both hands in her lap.

"I'm so sorry. I didn't mean to…" He could see her distraught expression in the profile of her face. "I almost raped you." She spat the words, shaking her head like she couldn't believe what she had done.

Michael couldn't help the smile that stretched his lips. "I think that's a bit too severe, don't you? I mean you just healed those parts of me, so I think you may be entitled to play with them."

Her gaze snapped back to his, showing a mixture of surprise and anger, and he realized that his words might easily be taken the wrong way. "I'm sorry." Frowning as he silently cursed his own stupidity, he put his hands up with his palms facing her. "That was a stupid joke. Uncalled for. Please forget I said that. I didn't mean to imply…anything."

Stephanie's gaze softened, and a small smile played on her lips. "Then we're both sorry. Can you forget that ever happened?"

Michael's cock was still as hard as a steel rod, and need was pulsing through his body. The feel of Stephanie's hand stroking him wasn't something he was likely to forget anytime soon. "Sure. No problem." Michael gave her a gentle smile and tried to will his member to calm down.

CHAPTER 3

Steph still felt embarrassment eating at her. The feel of his growing cock had utterly mesmerized her, the way it had lengthened and thickened against her palm. It was a long time since she had lost her virginity, and she'd had more than a few good bed partners, but she had never been with anyone like Michael. The size of his member when it finally stopped growing was mindboggling, and Steph was surprised that she hadn't started drooling.

Thankfully, Michael had snapped her out of her trance before her body had gone into full prep mode. He might have been able to smell her arousal, and that would have been even more mortifying.

Concentrating on not sneaking a peek at his package to see if he was still hard, she tried to come up with a safe topic of conversation. But her mind was stuck on one topic and didn't want to budge.

"Where did you learn to heal someone like that, or were you born with the ability?" Michael was staring at

her with a mixture of curiosity and amazement in his gaze. "I've heard stories about individuals being able to cure other people of disease, but none of them ever seemed legit."

She took a calming breath and held his gaze. "I've always been able to heal others, at least for as long as I can remember. I must've been about five when I found a squirrel that was struggling to move with a damaged leg. After petting it for a while, the squirrel took off running. I can't remember doing anything specific, but whatever I did seemed to improve its condition."

"And you've healed people as well, not just animals?"

"Yes, although…" Pausing, she thought back on the last time she had healed someone, and what a clusterfuck that had been. A boyfriend she had healed several years ago had tried to convince her to sell her services, and he got really pissed off when she wouldn't do it. He had viewed her abilities as his ticket to getting rich fast. Asshole. "It's a bit of a risk. You'd think people would be grateful and treat you nicely when you've just helped them, but my experience is that they either shun you or try to exploit you. I haven't used my power in several years."

Michael sighed and nodded. "Yeah, that's hardly surprising. Most people belong in one of two categories: those who fear what they can't understand or those who want to use it for their own gain." He looked at her more intently. "But why didn't you heal yourself up in the mountains? Or at least try after we managed to move the boulder?"

"I couldn't." Sadness and frustration filled her and

probably showed on her face. The hopelessness of her—and now Michael's—situation caused her shoulders to sag. "I've never been able to heal myself. If I had, I wouldn't be in this situation."

"And by this situation you mean whatever is going on with Jack and his brutes?" Michael's eyes darkened with anger.

Closing her eyes, Steph swallowed and tried to stop the tears from welling up. She had been in a bad situation for quite a while with Jack and his clan of panthers, but suddenly so was Michael. And it was all her fault. She was sure of it.

A hand gently covering hers made her open her eyes. Michael gave her a small warm smile, and the tears she had been trying to hold back overflowed and ran down her cheeks.

Before she knew it, Michael sat up and two strong arms came around her. His right hand cupped the back of her head, and she leaned her forehead against his upper chest. No words were spoken, and after a couple of minutes, she felt her despair start to ease.

Steph lifted her head and looked up into Michael's face. Noticing how close he was, she couldn't help her gaze dropping to his lips. They looked soft, and she wondered how it would feel to have him kiss her. The corners of his lips lifted in a grin, and she quickly raised her gaze to his. Amusement was shining in his eyes for a second before he looked away.

"Stephanie, we have to come up with a plan for when we stop." Michael returned his gaze to hers, but all traces of amusement were gone. "Do you know where we're going?"

She nodded. "I think so. We're probably going to

Jack's estate. The headquarters for his panther clan."

"So Jack's the clan alpha?"

Steph nodded again. "Yes."

"How much time do you think we've got before we get there?" Michael stared at her, his expression serious.

She thought about it for a few seconds before answering him. "About twenty minutes. I think. But I can't be sure. I lose my sense of time passing when I use my power."

**

Twenty minutes. Michael studied the woman in his arms. He had seen how her eyes had dipped to his lips earlier, and that she had been considering kissing him had been plainly written on her face. And he had just about given in and captured her full lips with his own. The only thing that had held him back was the fucked-up situation they were in.

At least Stephanie wasn't Jack's. There was no scent to indicate that she had been with Jack in an intimate sense the last couple of months, and she was definitely not a panther's mate. Michael would have been able to pick that up easily while holding her so close.

Twenty minutes, though. His thoughts should be on that. That was the time they had to prepare for whatever might happen when they arrived at the panthers' headquarters.

He stared into Stephanie's tear-filled hazel eyes and felt something clench in his chest. It might or might not have been his heart. The thought of what Jack and his brutes could do to her had him reeling, and Michael struggled to push the horrible images out of his mind so he could focus on coming up with a plan to save her from those assholes.

"Have you been to Jack's estate before?" He kept his expression as neutral as possible while stroking her back in what he hoped was a calming fashion.

She nodded. "Yes, I was kept there for close to four months before I managed to escape. Jack seemed so charming and considerate when I first met him. A bit old-fashioned maybe, but I let myself be fooled by his looks and charm. So stupid. So fucking stupid. I threw a tantrum when I realized that I wasn't allowed to leave, but that only brought out his violent side."

Michael felt his fur wanting to burst through his skin. Fury rolled through him at the thought of Jack hurting this beautiful, strong woman. Because she was strong, there was no doubt about that. Most people would just cower and do whatever was asked of them when faced with someone like Jack. But as far as Michael could determine, Stephanie never had.

"Do you know why he's holding you captive?" Michael couldn't come up with a good reason to hold her against her will. Stephanie wasn't a panther, so that wasn't it. She was beautiful, but Jack hadn't taken advantage of her sexually. And by the way she called him old-fashioned, it sounded like they'd never been intimate. Michael couldn't understand why Stephanie was so important to Jack, unless the bastard had found out about her power to heal.

The way she stiffened in his arms made Michael frown and study her face.

"He wants to mate me." Her voice was a low whisper, and a tremble ran through her body.

Michael froze. That wasn't what he had expected to hear. It didn't make sense. Why hadn't Jack mated her already if he'd had her for four months? "I'm sorry to have to ask you this, Stephanie, but why hasn't he mated you already if that's his intention?"

Her body sagged in his arms like she was about to give up, and Michael wanted to shake her and tell her to stay strong. This wasn't the time to give up, but she had been holding on for months, apparently, so at some point even she might break.

"It's supposed to happen on a specific day for some reason. I don't know why. That day is in two days."

"Fuck!" His animal side wanted to take over and fight, but Michael clamped down on that side of himself. Two days. He had to get her out of the damned panther's clutches within two days. Again, Michael regretted not calling James and giving him the information he had received from Chris. At least then there might have been a chance of someone rescuing them. Michael had left his phone in the rental car, and James would understand that something was amiss when Michael didn't contact him or answer his calls. But James wouldn't expect Michael to contact him until the next day, and that left precious little time for his friends to find them before the time was up. As it stood, his friends didn't even know where to begin searching.

Michael took a deep breath and tried to calm himself. "I think our time is almost up, and we don't know what will happen when we get to panther headquarters." Using one finger underneath her chin, he gently tipped her face up to his. The hopelessness in her gaze when it landed on him almost floored him, but he kept going with what he wanted to say to her.

"It's probably safe to assume that Jack won't

change his plans and try to mate you before the two days are up. No matter the reason he has chosen that specific day, it must be a good one since he's waited this long."

Michael continued when Stephanie only looked at him. "Without your healing power, I would still be in terrible pain, and when we arrive, I need to play into that. We can't let them know that I'm fine. Do you understand?"

She nodded.

"Pretending to still be down... They'll probably be more relaxed around me, and I might find out something that will help us get away."

Stephanie started shaking her head, and her eyes filled with fear. "No, Michael. Don't try anything. They'll hurt you again. Please."

He smiled down at her. It was endearing how concerned she was for his wellbeing after she herself had been living in hell for four months. "Stephanie. I won't do anything rash. I promise. First of all, I will try to gather as much information about the panthers and this estate as possible while pretending to still be hurt. They're unlikely to hurt me again as long as I don't show any signs of improvement. But you have to promise not to show any concern for me, no matter what they do. If they suspect for a second that you care, even a little bit, they'll hurt you. Or they'll hurt me to get to you."

She frowned at him and sighed. "I'll try, but if they hurt you like before, I'm not sure I'll be able to hide my concern. The shock prevented me from showing how it affected me last time, but if something like that happens again—"

Michael cut her off. "You have to. Or Jack will have a whole new reason to hurt you. I don't think he'll be very forgiving of you showing any interest in another man. And that's how he'll interpret your concern for me. He'll see me as a rival. And if something can trigger him to mate you early, that might do it."

He felt her jaw tense, and anger and defiance surfaced in her eyes. Michael silently cheered. He would much rather have her angry and defiant than full of fear and hopelessness.

"Stephanie." Michael couldn't help smiling at her despite everything.

"Please call me Steph. That's what my friends do." Her eyes were on his, and a small smile pulled at the corners of her mouth.

"Steph then."

Michael felt the van slowing down. Their time was up. Before he could think better of it, he pressed his lips gently to hers, and she let out a small moan. The sound made his cock twitch, but before he could fall for the temptation to deepen the kiss, he pulled away and looked at her.

"We'll get away. Somehow, I'll find a way to get us out of there before Jack can mate you. I promise." He let go of her and lay down. Curling into himself, he imitated the position he would be in if his balls were busted, literally.

Steph pulled away from him and lay down on the floor, taking care to place her broken leg up on some brown bags leaning against the wall.

She glanced over at him, and he winked at her before tucking his chin down against his chest.

CHAPTER 4

James hadn't been able to relax after speaking to Michael on the phone. He had a bad feeling about this. After he discussed the situation with Carlos at length, they both agreed they had to go back to Fort William and help Michael. The guy could come across as a dick at times, but deep down he was a decent guy who had grown up with a power-hungry asshole for a father.

The train would be pulling into Edinburgh in a few minutes, and James and Carlos needed to persuade their wives to stay in Edinburgh while they themselves rented a car and went back to Fort William. They had intentionally avoided speaking to their wives, Ann and Marna, on the train. James had no doubt that Ann would disagree with him about staying behind in Edinburgh, and he didn't want to make a scene on the train.

Ann and Marna were both human and could easily get hurt or killed, something James and Carlos were well aware of. Being mated to wereservals, the women had better chances of recovery when hurt than normal humans, but they were not nearly as resilient as wereanimals. And even if Ann had been a shifter, James wouldn't have wanted to bring her into a possible battle. The same went for Carlos with his wife.

The train pulled into the station and stopped, and they exited the train. They had booked hotel rooms not far from the station and opted to walk. While making their way through the streets of Edinburgh, James was trying out several options in his head for explaining the situation to Ann, but he realized that no matter what he said, she wouldn't accept being left behind without objections. Ann was fierce and did not back down if things got tough, but sometimes he wished she was a little bit more pliable. As soon as the thought crossed his mind, however, he knew it wasn't true. He had fallen in love with Ann exactly the way she was, and he didn't want her any other way.

As soon as they entered their hotel room and closed the door, James dropped the luggage he had been carrying on the floor. In two long strides, he covered the distance to his mate and pulled her into his arms. Kissing her deeply, he was tempted to forget about Michael and rather focus on undressing his wife, but instead he gently ended the kiss and took a step back.

Ann narrowed her eyes at him and crossed her arms. The move pushed her breasts up, and James had to make a conscious effort to keep his gaze on hers instead of letting it dip to her magnificent chest. This woman was his strength and his weakness. He would never get enough of her.

"Why do I get the feeling I'm not going to like what you're about to say?" Ann stared at him in defiance, already prepared to fight for her opinion.

James steeled himself for the coming discussion and launched into what he hoped would be a convincing speech.

"As you know, Michael got off the train in Fort William because he had something he wanted to do. I called him later, and he said he had seen Stephanie. She was hauled away by two men, and they took off in a gray van. Michael had someone run the license plate number of the van when I spoke to him, and he was planning to go after her. I made him promise not to get into anything without us, but I've got a bad feeling about this. Carlos and I need to go back to Fort William to support Michael. I'll make sure we only make some careful inquiries. Anything more will have to be handled by the police. But just to be on the safe side, we want you and Marna to stay here in Edinburgh." James stared at his wife and prayed she would heed his words for once.

"Okay, and Marna and I can't stay at a hotel in Fort William, why?" Ann was obviously annoyed, judging by the look on her face.

He decided to try a different tactic. "You and Marna will have some time to shop and see the sights here in Edinburgh. Shopping is not really my thing, as you well know, so I think this is a great solution. You can focus on what you would like to do here while we help Michael." James could hear how lame that sounded, and he almost cringed at his own weak reasoning.

"Great solution, my ass." Ann was glaring at him.

"And when something happens to you, and we have to get to Fort William quickly? I guess us driving while we're all agitated and scared is a good solution too?"

Ice filled his veins in horror at the thought of Ann in a car crash. His woman knew exactly what to say to render his arguments useless. He couldn't promise her nothing would happen to them while trying to find Stephanie's whereabouts. That would clearly be a lie. James was going to do his utmost to stay out of any conflicts, but there was always a small chance of it happening anyway.

Ann stepped up to him and pressed her lips against his in a short kiss. Putting her arms around his neck, she looked into his eyes and gave him a gentle smile. "We'll come with you to Fort William and find a hotel. Marna and I will stay there while you help Michael in his search for Stephanie. But… And this is nonnegotiable." She paused and her gaze sharpened. "I'll call Jennie and tell her about this. Perhaps Trevor and Duncan can help. I'd feel better if there were four of you instead of two, not to mention that they've got local knowledge and contacts that will make the job of finding Stephanie much easier."

And that was why James loved this woman. Beautiful, intelligent, and prepared to face anything that came her way.

∞∞∞∞

The door to the back of the van opened and Jack scowled at Steph. She met his eyes and sat up, reaching her arms out toward him to make sure he focused on her. Steph was determined to do anything in her power to keep Jack's attention on her instead of Michael. Hopefully, then, the likelihood of him attacking Michael again would be lower.

"My leg is quite sore. Will you help me? I know I'll be safe in your strong arms." Trying for an admiring expression she didn't feel, she hoped for the best. Jack was a sucker for adoration and anything that showed him as superior was welcome with him. It might even blind him a bit to anything else going on.

A smirk developed on Jack's face, and he actually seemed to stand a bit taller. "You should fucking remember that. As my mate you'll be envied by all the females in this clan, as well as most of the human females around here. It's about time you showed some fucking appreciation."

He picked her up and indicated to his goons to get Michael. Jack had one arm under her knees and one around her back as he carried her toward the main entrance of the large house. She put her arms around his neck and looked up into his face. Thinking about the way Michael had held her and the quick kiss he had given her just a few minutes ago helped her put more warmth into the smile she gave Jack.

The smirk was still on Jack's face, but he frowned when his eyes moved to her cheek. Steph could feel that she had a bruise from where his fist had landed. Asking about the drugs she had seen at the warehouse was the last in a long line of bad judgement calls on her part. She had to learn to stay her tongue, particularly since Michael's wellbeing was at stake.

"You have to stop making me hit you like that." Jack scowled at her, and she could almost feel his anger rising. "And you need to start putting on some weight. I want tits and ass that I can hold onto while I fuck you. A bag of bones doesn't get a male's blood flowing."

Steph could feel her fear rising as Jack's voice changed into more of a snarl with his anger. If she didn't do something to stop his temper from flaring, she would soon have another bruise somewhere.

"I'm so sorry, Jack. I know I'm not worthy of you. Can you please forgive me?" She let her fear and sense of hopelessness at her situation flood her, and tears welled in her eyes as a result. Leaning into him, she whispered close to his ear. "I'm scared, Jack. All those people at our mating. They'll be judging me, and I'm not good enough for you. They'll see. All of them. And they'll come for me and kill me because I'm not worthy of their king." Steph was laying it on thick and playing into the fear he could smell on her.

"Now don't you worry about that. Nobody will kill the panther king's mate. They wouldn't dare."

She couldn't see his face, but Steph could hear the satisfaction in Jack's voice. Being called king was something he had secretly wanted, just like she had suspected. She rested her head against his shoulder and tried to relax her body. "Thank you, Jack. I know I'm safe with you, and that you'll take care of me, but please understand that the mating ceremony is frightening for someone like me. I've never even been to one, so I don't know what to do to make sure I please you." Hopefully, that would explain her fear and anxiety, masking her concern for Michael.

"Just show them how good I make you feel. I'm going to do all the work, anyway, so you only have to be there. Nothing to it. And then I'll be king." Jack's chuckling was low and ominous.

Steph barely stopped her shiver of disgust and fear. Thankfully, nobody could see her face as she turned it into his shoulder. She didn't like the way he said he would be king. It almost sounded like Jack believed he was going to change with the mating, but she was probably just letting her imagination run away with her.

He carried her through the foyer and up the main staircase of the house. Moving her head a little to look over Jack's shoulder, she just caught the two assholes half carrying, half dragging Michael as they disappeared down the corridor to the right of the entrance. There were rooms down that way used for holding prisoners, so she wasn't surprised. What amazed her was that she herself wasn't going to be kept in one of them.

The room Steph had been using for the months she had been kept at the estate appeared to be exactly as she had left it. Her bed was still unmade, and a few pieces of clothing were scattered on the floor.

Jack lowered her legs to the floor and Steph held onto him for support. Before letting go of him, she looked up into his eyes and tried to infuse her voice with sincerity and admiration. "I know I don't deserve your help after what I've put you through, but do you think there are some crutches in this house that I can use? I need to put on some weight as you pointed out, and if I can get down to the kitchen on my own, it'll make it easier for me to eat often."

Jack narrowed his eyes at her, and she automatically braced for impact. But to her surprise, it only took a second before his expression smoothed out.

"About time you took some responsibility for your appearance. I'll have someone get you some crutches." He turned around and walked to the door.

"Thank you, Jack." And she meant that from the bottom of her heart. Crutches would help her get around. No long distance running for her for a while yet, but anything was better than nothing. And he hadn't even objected to her moving around the house.

The door closed, but there was no sound of a key turning in the lock. Steph did a mental fist pump. Not exactly a get out of jail free card but better than she had expected.

∞∞∞∞

The way Steph was sweet-talking Jack had Michael's skin prickling with how his fur wanted to erupt. And the asshole's derogatory comments about her body didn't help either. He would like nothing better than to attack the bastard and end him right this second, but Michael knew he would jeopardize their chances of escape if he acted too soon.

Michael kept his head down and studied his surroundings carefully as Jack's two brutes half dragged, half carried him into the house and down a corridor to the right. It was a huge house, but there wasn't a lot of people around. At least not at present.

They stopped outside a steel door, and the guy on Michael's left opened it to reveal a small cell with a cot against the right-hand wall. In the far-right corner at the head of the cot was a toilet and a wash basin.

Michael was dumped unceremoniously on the cot, and his left hand was cuffed to a length of chain fastened to a steel ring mounted on the wall right next to the bed. He estimated the chain to be long enough to allow him to get to the toilet but not much farther. The setup was well thought out, so it was clear that Michael wasn't their first prisoner.

"Shift and you'll find yourself in a cage instead. Your choice." The voice was rough from lack of use.

Michael didn't acknowledge the thug's message. He stayed in the near-fetal position he had adopted when they dumped him on the cot, trying to maintain the illusion that he was still in severe pain and was protecting himself from another possible hit to his genitals.

The door slammed shut, and Michael heard the sound of two people walking away down the corridor. He slowly opened his eyes to make sure he was alone. A careful glance around revealed the room in more detail. The floor, ceiling, and all four walls were bare concrete. A single bulb in the ceiling was the only source of light in the room. There were no windows and no furniture apart from the cot. The door appeared to be of a thick steel variety. In summary there was only one positive thing about his prison cell. There were no cameras. So whatever Michael did in the room would not be supervised by Jack or any of his people.

Michael stretched out on the cot and tried to make his body relax. There wasn't much he could do to get out of his cell. No doubt the place had been used for shifters before. He looked at the cuff and chain keeping his wrist locked to the wall. Sitting up on the cot, he stretched out his arm and applied some of his strength, but there was no give in the setup.

Lying back on the cot, Michael thought about his situation. His options were limited. To be able to escape, he had to get free of the chain and get through the door. Whether or not his captors intended to feed him was still a question, but if they did, he might get an opportunity to catch them by surprise. It would depend on who came into the cell with his food, and if the person had a key to the cuff he was wearing.

If they left him there without food for an extended length of time, the only possibility Michael could think of was to attract someone's attention in a manner that would cause them to open the door. Preferably a person with a key to the cuff. It was a long shot, but nothing was impossible. And if no other opportunities emerged, he would have to try it.

Another possibility might arise if they decided to remove him from the cell for some reason. Whether that would provide him with an opportunity to escape depended on a lot of factors, and he would have to be observant and play it by ear.

Regardless of his own chances of escape, there was another complicating factor in all of this. He wouldn't leave this place without Steph. Either Michael managed to find her and bring her with him when he left, or he would stay.

An image of beautiful hazel eyes gazing up at him came into his mind. She had looked tired and pale as she was healing him in the van, but she was still beautiful. There was something about Steph that caught his attention, and when he was with her, he found it hard to look away. He had never experienced anything like it before. No other woman had ever been able to hold his attention the way she did.

The feel of her hand stroking his length through his jeans had almost made him come right there on the floor of the van. Her gaze had been fixed on his crotch as his cock hardened, and Michael would never forget the mesmerized look on her face. He had removed her hand just in time to prevent spilling his seed in his pants. Just another couple of strokes, and he would have shot off like a rocket.

The memories had blood flowing to his cock, and his jeans grew tight as his swollen member strained against the material. The thought of Steph's soft lips against his own when he kissed her had his balls pulling up and need pounding through him. His body wanted release, but he couldn't obey its insistent demand. Not when he had to be prepared to exploit an opportunity for escape at a moment's notice.

Michael snapped open the button of his jeans and pulled down the zipper. His dick sprang free, and he moaned at the sensation. He pushed his jeans a little down his legs and used his hands to check his balls and cock for any remaining damage, all while listening for any movement outside indicating that someone was coming. It was good to be able to confirm that all his parts were fine, but it was torture touching himself like this and knowing that he couldn't risk bringing himself to orgasm. Particularly with the feel of Steph's hand on him so fresh in his mind. Her firm strokes had been heaven even through the fabric of his jeans, and Michael was convinced that her power had upped the feeling even more.

Sweat broke out across his forehead, and his heart was beating double time in his chest. His balls pulling up even tighter made him realize he had been stroking his cock while thinking of Steph. He squeezed his member right below the engorged head to stop his impending orgasm just as he heard footsteps moving toward his cell in the corridor outside. He could feel his muscles straining as his body was begging for release. Lifting his head from the cot, he thought the angry red head of his dick seemed to be staring at him in accusation at the discomfort.

The footsteps were getting closer, and Michael struggled to pull up his jeans and close it over his swollen member. He turned onto his side and curled his body around the injuries he was still pretending to be feeling acutely. His hard cock was digging painfully into the zipper of his jeans, but that couldn't be helped.

Michael listened carefully as the footsteps stopped outside his cell. A full minute went by without a sound, and whoever it was didn't open the door to his cell. Then the footsteps moved slowly away and disappeared.

He breathed out a sigh of both irritation and relief as he rolled over onto his back on the cot. If somebody had entered his cell, it might have presented Michael with an opportunity to escape, and losing the opportunity or at least postponing it, was frustrating. It was a relief, however, to be able to stretch out his body and let his still engorged member have a little more room. He wasn't about to open his jeans and let it spring free, though. It would be too tempting to let his fantasies of Steph take over and forget about everything else.

CHAPTER 5

They were on their way back to Fort William in a rental car. It would take about three hours, but at least they would be there by dark.

James was apprehensive about bringing his wife so close to a possible conflict, but then he understood her position as well. If something happened to him, she wanted to be close by.

He had tried calling Michael before they left Edinburgh, but after about twenty seconds, the call had gone to voicemail. Either Michael had left his phone somewhere or he was too busy to answer. James tried a second time, but the same thing happened. That was about an hour ago, and Michael had yet to call back.

"I'll call Jennie and see if I can get ahold of her."

His wife's voice from the backseat had James glancing at her in the rearview mirror. "Okay."

After a few seconds, he heard Jennie's voice as she answered the call.

"Hi, Ann. Have you all arrived safely in Edinburgh?"

"Yes, and I guess…no." There was amusement in Ann's voice.

"What do you mean no?"

"You're on speaker now, so everyone can hear us."

"Okay." James could almost hear how Jennie was frowning through the phone.

"We're on our way back to Fort William as we speak. Michael is already there." Ann was serious. Her previous amusement was gone.

"What? What's going on?"

Ann put her hand on James's shoulder, and he started to explain.

"Michael saw Stephanie from the train window as we were arriving in Fort William this morning. Two guys put her in a gray van and took off. They didn't seem to care about her, and from what I can understand from talking to Michael, she didn't go with them by choice. Michael got off the train to try to intercede, but they were already driving off in the van by the time he got there."

"Did he get the license plate number?" Trevor's deep voice sounded through the phone.

"He did, but he never gave it to me." James silently cursed himself for not asking Michael to send it to him. "And now I can't get ahold of Michael on the phone. I think he might've found the owner of the van and is already off trying to find Stephanie."

"But it was a gray van you said, close to the train station?" James could almost feel Trevor's alpha power over the phone. Trevor was an extremely powerful alpha wolf shifter. One of the most powerful alphas

James had ever met.

"Yeah, that's all I know. Not much to go on I'm afraid. We'll start asking around when we get there. Someone might've noticed the same as Michael, and hopefully we can get some more information that way."

"There's bound to be surveillance cameras in that area. We know the time and place. I'll get someone on it immediately. I'm sure we'll have something by the time you arrive in Fort William. Duncan and I will meet you there." Trevor was nothing if not resourceful.

"Thank you, Trevor. Your help is very much appreciated." They said their goodbyes, and James breathed a silent sigh of relief. He had been worried about Michael since not reaching him on the phone earlier, but after talking to Trevor, James felt more confident that they would find him.

"Thank fuck. I was wondering how we were going to find Michael if he's managed to get himself into trouble." Carlos spoke from the passenger seat. "Now we might actually have a chance."

James glanced over at his friend and chuckled. "Yeah, my thoughts exactly."

∞∞∞∞

Steph was lying on the bed in her room, resting. Her broken leg was elevated to reduce the swelling, but the pain was still intense. Not really any surprise there with everything that had happened to her in the last twelve hours. She debated trying to get to her dresser to find some painkillers, but the effort required was too much to contemplate at the moment. Instead, she tried to forget about the pain by letting her mind wander to a more handsome topic.

Michael's lips on hers had come as a surprise, but they had left a lasting impression and a hunger for more. And she had a feeling that it would have developed into a more passionate kiss if they had more time. But time was exactly what they didn't have, and Steph regretted that fact even more since meeting Michael again. She couldn't think of a more perfect specimen of a man than him. A man she could actually see herself with for longer than a few weeks.

He was handsome with his classic features, but his warm light-brown eyes pushed him up the scale to gorgeous. And that body. She could only imagine how he would look with his shirt off, as she had never seen him without clothes. He would be a sight to behold. Steph had no doubt.

Remembering the feel of his cock growing under her hand had her sucking in a breath as her body clenched in response. Steph had been so mesmerized by the size and feel of his member that she hadn't realized what she was doing until he grabbed her wrist. His rod was larger than she had ever encountered with any of her previous lovers and one-night stands. In fact, she was wondering if he would even fit inside her. She would have to be really wet, and with some careful thrusting, he might be able to inch inside her slowly. Just the thought had her squeezing her legs together, as her clit started throbbing and her channel started leaking in preparation for such an event.

Steph abruptly sat up to try to dislodge the train of thought she was on. She needed to focus on how to get Michael away from Jack, not fantasize about the man's large cock.

One thing she was wondering about was how Michael had come to be at Jack's warehouse. The only thing she had told Michael when she met him up in the hills was her first name. So it was a bit of a surprise when he was suddenly there when she woke up after Jack had hit her and rendered her unconscious. Was it a coincidence, or was Michael there to save her from Jack? In the van he had promised to get her away from the asshole, but Steph wasn't sure if that proved that Michael had come looking for her specifically. Because how the hell could he, when he didn't know her full name or who had taken her? She would really like to believe that Michael had been actively looking for her and somehow managed to find her, but it was more likely that it was a coincidence. And that left an uncomfortable question. Why had Michael visited Jack's warehouse if he wasn't there for her?

Steph shook her head. She didn't want to speculate about Michael's reasons for being at the warehouse. It was better to ask him if she got the chance. No amount of musing would get her the answers she sought.

A knock on her door broke her out of her contemplations.

"Yes, come in." Steph kept her eyes on the door as it opened, and one of Jack's goons took a step across the threshold. She braced and prepared to defend herself, but then she saw what was in his hands. Crutches.

"Oh, thank you. Those will help me get down to the kitchen." They would help her move around the rest of the house and outside as well, but that was better left unsaid.

He left the crutches leaning against her bed, gave her a short nod, and left.

Steph didn't waste any time grabbing the crutches and using them to get to her dresser. First things first—painkillers. She brought a couple of the pills into the adjoining bathroom and filled a glass of water. While she swallowed the pills, her eyes landed on herself in the mirror. She looked just as tired and pale as earlier that day, and the bruise on her cheek did nothing to improve her appearance. But what caught her eye was her lank hair and grimy tank top. Her leg was killing her, but she desperately wanted a shower.

Using the crutches, she exited the bathroom and went back to her dresser. After digging through a couple of drawers, she found a pair of loose-fitting shorts. It was the only thing she had that would fit with her leg in a cast, except for the baggy pants she was wearing.

Steph made several trips from her room to the bathroom, gathering everything she required for her shower. Two chairs, a large plastic bag and a thin belt. When she was finally seated in the shower with her leg resting on a chair and wrapped in plastic, she had to take a minute to relax and focus on her breathing to combat the pain. Hopefully, the painkillers would start working soon.

The long shower worked wonders for both her body and mind. Her situation hadn't improved any, but at least she felt clean and refreshed. And the painkillers had started to kick in, so there was that.

Sitting on the chair in front of the mirror and

plaiting her hair, she planned her trip down to the kitchen. Eating was important to increase her energy and strength, but Steph also had other tasks planned for the evening. But first, food.

Arriving in the large kitchen, she found there was already a couple of women there preparing enough food for what looked like a lot of people. They both nodded at Steph when she entered the room, but they did nothing to hide the disdain and anger in their expressions. Most of the women in the clan would have done just about anything to take her place as Jack's mate, and they made no secret of their anger and disbelief at him choosing Steph to be his mate. She had been disrespectful and even downright hostile toward him since she arrived at the estate, and worst of all she wasn't a panther shifter. Why Jack chose her was a mystery to those women, just as it was to Steph.

While keeping her distance from the women, she prepared her food and packed it in containers. Then she got a juice carton from the fridge and put it all in the backpack she had brought with her from her room.

Steph was just exiting the kitchen when she almost crashed into Jack in the doorway. His face was blank as he stared at her, but she tried to give him a small smile to play nice. Anything she could do to placate the man was worth the effort while Michael was in the house. At least then her actions wouldn't cause him any additional pain.

"Have you eaten?" Jack kept his eyes on her.

"Not yet." Steph turned a little to show him the backpack she was carrying. "But I've made food to bring to my room. I'll eat there. I don't want to disturb whatever you've got planned for this evening."

Jack narrowed his eyes at her. "How do you know I've got plans?"

Steph gave him a neutral expression and nodded at the women in the kitchen. "They're preparing a lot of food. It's not a stretch to assume that you're having important guests tonight." Hopefully, he would understand that it was the normal assumption to make, and that she hadn't been snooping around. It was hard to tell with Jack sometimes, what would set him off.

He nodded. "Yes, you might as well know. Representatives from the other panther clans will be arriving soon. They will be present at our mating ceremony, and I'll be preparing them for that. Afterward, we've got some panther business to discuss."

Steph swallowed. Even more people that would be present at their mating. She had to quickly push it out of her mind in order to stay calm and not succumb to a panic attack.

Jack's expression changed into one of anger as he let his gaze scan her body from head to toe. "I don't want to see you near the conference room or anywhere else where you can be seen by one of our guests. Understood? You look weak and your injury… Well, we'll see what we can do about that in the morning."

Steph was left standing in the kitchen doorway when Jack turned around and stalked off. What did he mean by that? She shook her head and used her crutches to get to her room. Perhaps he was considering possibilities to conceal her injury, but how that was supposed to work she had no idea. No matter what was done to hide the cast, she still couldn't get around on her own without the crutches.

It was a relief not having to attend Jack's meeting, however. Steph didn't want to be involved in any panther or business-related activities of Jack's, particularly after what she had witnessed at the warehouse. Drugs of all things. It made sense. She just hadn't considered that he could be involved in something like that.

But the part about staying out of sight this evening fit right into her plans. Jack had visitors quite often, but she was rarely required to attend, in large part because of her attitude toward Jack and his plans for her. With visitors came additional security. Jack would keep several guards with him at all times, and the rest would be stationed at specific places in the house and around the estate grounds. There would be additional security outside patrolling the grounds, making it difficult to know where the guards were at any given time. Those were all things she had taken into account when preparing for her escape last time.

The positive side was that the guards inside the house would either be shadowing Jack or posted in the wing of the house where the conference room was located. There would be no security anywhere else in the house, giving her ample opportunity to stroll, or limp in her case, around those parts. And that aligned perfectly with her plans for the evening.

∞∞∞∞

Michael was lying on the cot, going through the details of his capture and what he had been able to see of the house. It was a large house situated on what he would expect to be an extensive property. He hadn't been able to catch but a glimpse of the grounds surrounding the house as he was hauled from the van, but what he remembered seeing were trees. The estate seemed to be located in a forest, and that might be to their advantage if he managed to get out of the house with Steph. He had no knowledge of the security in and around the place, however, but Steph probably had a fair idea since she had already been able to escape once. Although, her escape was likely to have provoked a change in the security routines, so they would have to be prepared for every scenario.

He sighed. This was fucked up, and he had done his part to fuck it up even more. If he had only made sure to have backup and relay everything he knew to James before he entered the warehouse, he and Steph would be better off than they were at the moment. But, no, Michael had opted to act alone, thinking it was better to carry it out as a stealth operation. He had been cocky and stupid, totally underestimating his opponents. Of course, he hadn't known that he was up against shifters, but he should have assumed a worst-case scenario and adopted a conservative approach.

The sound of footsteps approaching in the corridor had him turning over onto his side again. Curling in on himself, he waited as the person moved toward his cell. The footsteps were lighter this time, indicating a smaller person was approaching, perhaps a woman.

His cell door opened, and Michael opened his eyes a fraction to peek at the person entering. A petite woman with curly, long black hair took a step across the threshold. She was carrying a tray with food and a tall glass of water. Her gaze landed on him lying on the cot, and he tried to convey his pain as he opened his eyes fully and met her stare. She was pretty, with a pale porcelain complexion and big blue eyes. In another time and place, he would have made an effort to gain her as a lover, but not at the moment. The thought didn't even appeal to him.

The woman's eyes widened as she studied his face and body, and Michael gave her a small smile to encourage her reaction to him. Not too big a smile since he was supposed to be in pain, but enough to pique her interest.

Several seconds went by before she looked away, and a small blush crept up over her face. She put the tray down by his feet on the cot and abruptly turned and disappeared out the door. Michael was just opening his mouth to call her back when he realized she had left the door open. But before he could cheer at his lucky break, she was back with a small table. After putting the tray on the table, she carefully rolled it toward him while eyeing the chain restricting his reach. Michael discarded the possibility of grabbing the woman and checking for a key to the cuff on his wrist and decided on a different approach.

"Thank you for the food. It looks good." Michael kept the small smile on his face and hoped she would meet his gaze again. Her eyes snapped to his with an expression of astonishment on her face like she wasn't accustomed to someone thanking her.

Michael decided to press on while he had an advantage. "Do you think it would be possible to have a bar of soap and a towel? It would be nice to be able to clean up a little."

Her brows furrowed as if she didn't know how to

respond to his request.

"Only if it's okay of course, and it doesn't get you into any trouble."

She let her eyes sweep over his disheveled appearance before she nodded. "I think that will be okay." Her voice was a barely audible whisper. The next instant she was out the door, and it closed firmly behind her.

Michael listened as she moved down the corridor. He let another minute go by before he sat up and started eating. There was no telling when the woman would be back with the towel and soap, so Michael took his time eating. Devouring his food while being in agony would seem strange. That kind of pain would usually have caused him to lose his appetite, but he needed his strength and would eat the food given to him regardless of the impression it would give his captors.

Half an hour went by before the woman came back. She put the towel and soap by his feet on the cot and carefully extracted the table with the empty dishes without moving too close to him. Michael thanked her again, and she gave him a shy look and a nod before she quickly left.

CHAPTER 6

Trevor and Jennie were standing with Duncan outside the hotel in Fort William when they arrived. Duncan was a friend of Trevor and a wolf shifter as well. They were both big and built and automatically commanded respect, even though Duncan always seemed to have an amused expression on his face.

Ann had managed to secure a couple of rooms for the four of them for the night. Whether they would get much sleep that night, though, James had no idea.

They all got out of the car and quickly decided to move their conversation inside to one of their hotel rooms. After checking in they all filed into a room where their conversation was least likely to be overheard. It was a corner room with the only room adjoining it being the other room they had booked.

Everyone settled around the room on the bed and the available couch and chairs, and Trevor launched into giving them a summary of the information he had been able to gather so far.

"The gray van is a rental, and the company on the lease is owned by Jack Williams. He's the alpha of the local panther shifter clan and a well-known asshole. He has several businesses registered to him, and I can almost guarantee that he's involved in some illegal shit. It might be drugs, or it might be something else. I don't know."

Trevor sighed and continued. "Whatever Stephanie is mixed up in is nothing good, and I'm sorry to say this, but Michael doesn't stand a chance against this clan. They're brutal. If we're going to attempt to find and extract Stephanie and Michael, we should get some more help."

"Fuck!" James had been afraid that Stephanie was mixed up with something bad, but it was much worse than he had expected. He glanced at his wife and saw that she had gone pale.

James swung his gaze back to Trevor. "Anything else you can tell us?"

Trevor nodded. "There's a warehouse belonging to Jack's company right here in Fort William. It might be worth checking out. Then there's the estate about forty minutes north of here that serves as the clan's seat of power. I think Jack himself lives there, and they use it as a base for all their clan activities. It's a large property with the main house located in a forested area. I've got someone searching for details of the security setup for the place as we speak."

"Any other properties worth checking out?" Carlos was sitting on the bed next to his wife, who was just as pale as Ann.

"None that's close." Trevor looked at Carlos before sliding his gaze back to James. "There's a warehouse in

Inverness and a residential property in Perth, but if I was Jack, I'd keep my prisoners at the estate. Secluded, security measures in place, and full of loyal shifters. In other words, perfect."

"And damn hard to break into by the sounds of it." James sighed.

"I don't like this. It's too big a risk." James felt a hand clamp down on his arm and turned to see Ann staring at him, her eyes wide with fear.

He took her other hand in his and held her gaze. "We won't rush into this, I promise. We'll think things through and come up with a good plan."

James let his eyes travel around all the other faces in the room. They all nodded in response to his words to Ann.

∞∞∞∞

Steph ate and relaxed for a couple of hours before it was time to get on with her plan. She had been out of her room twice, checking on the status of Jack's meeting, after she'd brought her food back. Unseen to the visitors, she had watched from the upstairs landing as people arrived and were taken to the wing of the house where the conference room was located.

Moving carefully down the hallway in the opposite direction of the conference room, she did not encounter anyone. Being completely silent wasn't possible with her crutches, but she tried to keep the sounds of her moving around to a minimum. Steph wasn't barred from moving around the house this far from Jack's guests, but it was crucial that nobody knew where she was going.

Jack was a despicable asshole, but he had one redeeming quality. He was old-fashioned and didn't trust new technology. She suspected that he was terrified of leaving electronic footprints that could be spread on the internet, and that was why there were no CCTV or motion sensors around the estate. He simply used guards, mostly panther shifters, but she had also seen people from a guard service company from time to time. And she was quite sure that none of them were allowed to bring smartphones onto the property.

After carefully hopping down the back stairs to the ground floor, she turned and headed down the corridor toward the prison cells. There were three of them, and she had no idea which one they had put Michael in, but she was sure he was in one of them. The question was whether the other cells were empty or not. Steph hoped they were, but she had no way of telling other than opening them and checking.

She moved to the first prison cell and carefully extracted the key from her shorts pocket. It was a special type of key and the only reason she had one was that she had managed to steal it a couple of months back. Afraid she might end up being locked in one of the cells herself, Steph had managed to acquire one after two weeks of keeping an eye on the people attending the prisoners. She had found out that the keys were kept in a drawer in the kitchen. Knowing that, stealing one was easy, and she had never been questioned about it. Jack probably didn't think it likely that she was the culprit, considering she had no reason to want to use the cells or brake anyone out of them. And he had been right, until Michael came along.

She put the key in the lock, turned it, and then

opened the door a fraction. The room was dark, but the light from the corridor let her see that the cot visible through the crack in the door was empty. Steph swung the door open and quickly confirmed that there was nobody in the room. Breath left her in a whoosh, and she realized that she had been holding it in apprehension of what she would find in the room.

Steph locked the cell door and moved on to the next one. Repeating the procedure, she stared through the narrow crack at the cot. Michael was lying curled up on his side like he was in pain, and she felt her heartrate increase in alarm. Had they hurt him again?

She swung the door open and verified there was no one else in the room with him before quickly entering the cell and then locking the door behind her.

"Steph?" Worry laced his voice as Michael said her name softly. "You shouldn't be here. What if someone comes to check on me? Or they wonder where you are and start searching."

She smiled as she turned around and let her eyes scan him from top to toe. He didn't look like he was in pain, and she realized he had been faking it because he didn't expect it to be her opening his cell door.

"Don't worry. They're all busy in a different section of the house. I won't be missed, and nobody will come here. Jack has an important meeting with some other panther clans."

Michael frowned. "Are you sure? I don't want to cause you any more trouble."

Steph almost laughed outright but managed to stop herself in time. Grinning and shaking her head, she gazed into Michael's startled light-brown orbs. "You, cause me trouble? I've managed that very well on my own, and you had nothing to do with it. All you've done is help me."

She sat down beside him on the cot and frowned as one of her earlier questions popped into her mind. "Why were you at Jack's warehouse?" Steph wanted to ask him specifically if he was involved in the drug trade, but she refrained. She realized she really didn't want to know if he was. It would be devastating. But before she could tell him not to answer her question, he spoke.

"For you." Michael looked at her like it should have been obvious.

A sigh of relief escaped her, and she felt like laughing again. "Thank the stars. I was starting to worry that you were one of Jack's drug traders or something."

Michael lifted an eyebrow at her as his lips thinned, and she backpedaled. Steph didn't want to give him the impression that she thought him capable of something like that. "Not really, you know. Just, I didn't understand how you could be there for me. How did you find me? You knew nothing about me or who had taken me?"

His lips stretched into a grin at her flustered speech. "I was lucky actually. We were on our way to Edinburgh on the train, and I happened to see two assholes hauling you into a gray van." His grin changed into a scowl as he spoke. "I got off the train, but by the time I reached the parking lot, the van was driving off."

"But that doesn't explain how you found me at the warehouse."

"I'm getting to that. Have a little patience." A smile

played on his lips.

Steph couldn't help the way her eyes zoned in on those lips and stayed there. They were soft and had felt so good against hers. The kiss they had shared was just a quick peck. She wouldn't mind trying that again and going a bit further this time.

"Steph, are you listening to me?" Michael's voice was tinged with laughter, and she realized she had completely missed what he had been saying.

Feeling herself blushing she looked away. "Um, I... I'm sorry. I..." Steph didn't know what to say, and she didn't know why. It was a long time since she had acted like this with a man she liked. Almost like she was a teenager again.

The cot moved as Michael sat up. She felt his hand on her cheek, gently turning her face back to him. Her heartrate sped up as their gazes met, and she saw the heat in his eyes.

"I was saying that I caught the license plate number of the van and that's how I ended up at the warehouse." He stared at her lips while he spoke.

Steph barely caught the meaning of his words, she was so focused on his lips. The way they moved as he spoke had her almost in a trance.

Then he leaned toward her, and she held her breath as his mouth closed in on hers.

The first brush of his lips on hers had tingles racing through her body, and she couldn't help the moan that escaped from her. It seemed to spur him on, and their kiss turned more passionate quickly. She parted her lips, and their tongues tangled in a frenzied dance as their hands started exploring each other's bodies.

Steph let her hands glide over his chest and

shoulders. Hard, corded muscles played under her palms, and she could feel her body starting to weep for him. She let her hands follow his sides down to his waist before lifting his shirt to find bare skin. A shiver ran through his body as she touched his lower abs and let her fingers explore the pronounced ridges of his stomach.

His hands were doing a number on her as well. They had moved underneath her T-shirt and slid up to fondle the sides of her breasts. It was heaven and frustration combined. His hands felt so good on her, but she wanted him to cup her twins and fondle her nipples.

When he suddenly pulled away, she was left gasping for breath.

"I'm sorry." Michael's voice was a low rasp, and desire burned in his eyes. "I'd like nothing better than to keep kissing you, but we can't get carried away. If someone comes, we need to be prepared. I can't focus on anything else when I'm kissing you like that."

Steph sighed in frustration, but she liked his words about losing focus when kissing her. Michael was right, though. She was almost one hundred percent sure that nobody would come. But they couldn't risk it.

She nodded at the cuff on his wrist. "I'm sorry, but I don't have a key for that. I didn't realize that you would be chained to the wall, so I didn't know to look for a key. But I'll find it or something to cut the chain, and I'll come back later. Maybe tomorrow, when Jack doesn't have visitors. There are always extra guards patrolling the property when he has guests."

"Be careful, Steph." Concern was evident on Michael's face. "I don't want you risking yourself for me. It's better if you focus on getting yourself out of here. I'll give you my friend James's phone number. Contact him when you're safe, and he'll find a way to help me."

She scowled at him and shook her head. "No, I'm not leaving you here. Anything can happen to you. What if Jack hurts you again?" Her gaze dropped to his lap as she spoke and sucked in a breath when she saw the huge bulge in his pants. Apparently, she wasn't the only one who had been seriously turned on by their heated kisses.

Her channel clenched, and she whimpered as her clit started throbbing. Her whole body was preparing for Michael to have his way with her. And what did she have to lose? If everything turned out the way Jack planned, Steph would be mated in two days, and she would never be able to spend any more time with Michael. This might be her only chance.

CHAPTER 7

The whimpering sound Steph made when she saw the bulge in his pants went straight to Michael's cock, causing it to throb with anticipation. He felt his willpower crumble. He couldn't remember ever wanting a woman so badly before, and it wasn't just a need for release, although his body was screaming for that too. He wanted to make Steph feel good, to feel her body tremble with pleasure and taste her release on his tongue.

Before he realized what was happening, he was helping Steph as she removed his shirt. Her hands gliding over his bare skin had him groaning.

Her shirt hit the floor next, and he leaned back to get a good look at her. He admired the smooth skin covering her flat stomach and the tops of her breasts, before raising his gaze to hers. Keeping his eyes on hers, he reached behind her and slowly unhooked the fastenings of her bra. The desire in her eyes had him wanting to hurry, but he made himself slow down to really savor her.

Her small pert breasts came free of their cover, and Michael's balls pulled up in response as heat rushed through him. Then he scooted over on the cot and pulled her up to lie on her back beside him.

He arranged the chain connecting him to the wall to avoid pulling it across her body. Leaning over her, he kissed her lips and let his left hand glide up to cover a soft globe. He rolled her nipple between his fingers and smiled against Steph's lips when she moaned and arched her back to press her breast more firmly into his hand.

"So responsive," he murmured as he kissed his way down her jaw and neck to her clavicle. He moved his mouth to the breast he had been neglecting so far and proceeded to tease her nipple with his lips and tongue.

"Holy hell." Steph's voice was husky, and she was squirming.

He raised up on all fours above her and stared down into her flushed face. Her lips were a bit swollen from their kisses, and her eyes was so filled with desire his cock hardened up even more.

Her fingers were suddenly fiddling with the button on his jeans, and he looked down just as it snapped open. She slowly undid the zipper, and when his cock finally sprang free, his whole body jerked in response.

Michael heard Steph gasp, and he raised his gaze to her face to see her wide eyes as she stared at his swollen member.

"You're so big." Her voice was breathy, and she licked her lips.

He damn near came as he watched her tongue move over her swollen lips. The image of her looking at him like that was the most erotic thing he had ever seen.

"Will you fit inside me? I mean, you're really huge, you know. I'm willing to try, though. More than willing."

Her words made his cock twitch in anticipation, but there was still a smidgen of sense in his brain.

"I'd fit, but I can't… We're not going to be able to…" He stumbled and had to try again. "I can't come inside you. Jack will be able to smell me on you."

Steph frowned up at him. "Are you sure?"

Michael nodded. "Very sure."

"Well, you'll have to pull out before you come then. I can finish you with my mouth." Steph smiled like she had found the perfect solution.

He shook his head. "I can't risk being inside you at all. And coming anywhere in or on your body will leave a scent that Jack will be able to pick up. I'm sorry, Steph. But I can make you come with my mouth. In fact, I really want to taste you as you climax."

Her jaw went slack at his words, and she squeezed her legs together. Then she frowned and looked angry all of a sudden.

Michael was a bit taken aback until she spoke, and he understood why she looked angry.

"But that's not good enough. I want you to come as well."

"I'd love to come, Steph. Preferably while I'm inside you and can feel your body tighten around my cock as you climax."

"Yeah, that." She was staring at him in awe.

Michael felt her hand close around his shaft, and he

hissed at the incredible feeling of her soft hand on him.

"Steph," he croaked, hardly able to say her name as need stronger than he had ever felt before pounded through him.

"Just let me touch you for a little while. Please?"

"I'm close to coming. It won't take much." His words were breathy and staccato as he felt her hand glide slowly up and down his hard cock from root to tip. It was exquisite torture and a memory that would stay with him for the rest of his life.

Michael suddenly jerked out of her grasp. He squeezed his eyes closed as he clamped his fist around his straining shaft right below the bulbous head, tightened his grip to the point of pain to stop himself from coming all over Steph's body. He had let it go too far, almost to the point of no return. And he was paying the price. His balls were screaming in protest, and his shaft was throbbing with the sharp urge to spill his seed.

When the need to come relented a bit, he opened his eyes to find Steph staring at him.

"I'm sorry. That looked painful. You should've just turned away from me instead of squeezing your cock like that. Poor thing."

Michael followed her gaze as it moved to his shaft, and he had to agree with her. His rod was dark red and angry-looking. The head was visibly throbbing and as big as he had ever seen it.

He looked back at Steph and shook his head. "It can't be helped. If I'd spilled just one drop on you, it might've been enough to give off a scent. I couldn't risk it."

Steph's arms came up and pulled his head down to her for a kiss. Then she stared up at him with tears in her eyes. "You're too nice. How can you be this wonderful?"

He felt the corners of his mouth curl up into a smile and his heart soar from her words. The simple answer was that Steph was special. Michael had never met anyone like her before, and he wanted her with him, he realized, for the rest of his life. Not because he needed to find a woman to mate. Michael wanted her for her, in his life and in his bed, forever. The realization was fantastic and horrible at the same time. He had found his mate, but she was going to be mated to another shifter in two days.

One thing he knew was that he couldn't tell her. Firstly, she might not want a mate after what she had been through, even if they by some miracle managed to escape from Jack and his panthers. Secondly, if she felt the same attraction for him as he felt for her, she would be devastated to know that she was Michael's mate if she ended up mating Jack. The knowledge would cause her additional suffering, and he just couldn't put her through that.

"I want to watch you come."

Steph's voice pulled him back from his thoughts, and he took in her determined expression.

"No, as I said—"

She cut him off as she shook her head. "No, listen to me. I want you to make yourself come in front of me. I just want to watch. It would turn me on."

Staring at her, he could see that she meant it. Desire shone in her eyes and her heartrate was speeding up.

"Really? You want to watch me jerk off?"

Michael grinned when Steph nodded enthusiastically.

"Fuck if that isn't a turn-on. You have to stay far away from me, okay? And I'll make sure I don't spray everywhere."

He got off the bed and removed his pants. Before he could move away, Steph grabbed his cock and moved her hand gently up and down. Her other hand reached between his legs and started fondling his balls. It felt so good he didn't want to move away, but he was too close to let her keep going.

Michael closed his own hand over hers and gently removed it from his engorged member while looking into her eyes. She let go of his balls and sat back on the cot.

"Please move a little farther away from me." He indicated down at the end of the cot by the door. Then he moved over to the toilet. Stopping in front of it, Michael stood with his side to Steph. His hand closed around his member, and he turned his head toward her as he started moving his hand quickly up and down. Her eyes were riveted on his cock, and Michael could see her chest moving with her elevated breathing.

Her right hand disappeared down inside her shorts, and the hoarse moan that escaped from her mouth as she obviously started playing with herself had him tipping over the edge. Michael clamped his other hand over the head of his shaft as his seed started pumping out. The orgasm exploded through him, and the pleasure was so intense his knees almost buckled. The sight of Steph's obvious enjoyment at watching him orgasm prolonged his pleasure, and his whole body was shaking with the exertion when he finally started to come down.

Steph was still moving her hand inside her shorts and beathing heavily.

***

Steph was sliding the pad of her finger over her clit in tight circles, before moving her hand down and pumping a finger inside herself a few times. Then she moved her finger back to her clit. The sight of Michael jerking off had turned her on immensely, but Steph hadn't been able to come yet. Her finger felt small and inadequate after she saw his large cock. It just wasn't enough.

"Please let me do that for you." Michael had been staring at her since he first started fisting his member and all through his orgasm. His eyes had been switching between their normal light-brown color and an almost yellow hue. And she took the color change as a confirmation that he was a shifter.

At the moment his eyes were fixed on the junction of her thighs. "I'll just clean up, and I'll be right there. Please remove your shorts and lie down on your back for me. I want to spread you wide open."

Her pussy clenched at his words, and Steph did as he asked. She lay down on her back on the cot with her head toward the door.

Michael finished washing and turned around. He groaned as his eyes zeroed in on her down there. Before she even saw him move, he was on his hands and knees above her. Sliding his hands underneath her ass, he held her gaze while lowering his head toward her center.

His tongue licked all the way up her slit and over her clit, and she moaned at the sensation. He circled her clit several times, not quite touching it, before crossing it slowly with his tongue vibrating. Steph had no idea how he managed to do that, but it felt fantastic. He repeated the set of actions several times, starting with licking up her slit and ending with crossing her clit with his vibrating tongue.

Steph noticed that she was panting and making soft mewling sounds, as his tongue vibrated across her clit and brought her to the brink of orgasm. She was lifting her pelvis trying to make him keep going a little longer, but just as she was about to tip over into oblivion, he stopped and moved away from her clit. The same thing happened several times, and Steph was soon going crazy with the need to come.

"Michael, please."

He chuckled. "So impatient."

A finger breaching her entrance made her gasp. Curving his finger up to massage the sensitive front wall inside her, he pumped his finger in and out a few times. Then he added a second digit and increased the pace of his movements.

His tongue was back to licking her clit as he kept moving his fingers inside her, and she tried to close her thighs at the powerful sensations. But Michael's shoulders were in the way, and all she achieved was having him chuckle against her clit. The vibration took her to the edge, but just like before, he moved away before she tipped over.

"Michael. I need to come. Now!" Steph hissed, and her fists were in his hair trying to urge him to do what she needed of him.

This time he obeyed. His fingers started pumping in and out of her at a furious pace as his tongue vibrated firmly against her clit. Her eyes went wide, and her jaw slackened as the pleasure gathered in a ball in her lower belly ready to unleash. The orgasm erupted through her with pleasure more intense than she had ever felt before. Wave after wave rolled through her, and just as the tide was starting to ebb, Michael bit down gently on her clit, and another powerful orgasm washed through her. The pleasure shook her body with exquisite sensations. By the time she came down, she felt boneless, and she was struggling to find her words.

"I hope that was as good as it seemed. I'd love to taste you again and give you more pleasure, but I'm getting worried that someone will decide to come check on me."

More pleasure. Holy fuck. She didn't think she could handle any more.

Steph swallowed. "Thank you, Michael. That was…unreal." She moved her head to look at him.

He had moved from between her legs and was sitting with his back against the wall by her feet. His hand was caressing her knee.

She sat up and took in the magnificence of his naked body. Tall and lean with hard muscles. Wishing she had time to kiss and lick every inch of him, she let her eyes take in the details of him to commit to memory.

Her gaze stopped as it landed on his cock. It was fully erect and pointing toward the ceiling.

Michael chuckled, and her eyes snapped up to his.

"Yeah, I want you. Jerking off wasn't enough to quell the craving I've got for you. Not nearly enough."

"But you just came. How can you be this hard this

fast after…" Steph swallowed. Her channel clenched at the sight of him, even though only a minute ago she had thought she wouldn't be able to handle any more pleasure. Suddenly, all she could think of was straddling him and taking him inside her weeping channel. The way she ached for him had her squeezing her thighs together to try to get some relief, but it only had the opposite effect.

Heat burned in Michael's gaze as he stared at her. "Steph, I wish…" He stopped and closed his eyes. The expression on his face was one of defeat for just a second, before he opened his eyes and pasted a smile on his face.

She wasn't fooled. He wanted her, and their situation was hurting him just as badly as it was hurting her. It had been all there on his face for a second.

"You'd better go, Steph. I've enjoyed our time together immensely, but I'm getting worried that someone will come and find you here with me." As he spoke, he got off the cot and started pulling on his pants. Wincing, he barely managed to close his jeans over his straining shaft.

Sighing in resignation, she found her clothes and put them on. "I'll come back tomorrow and check on you. And I'll find that key." She nodded at the cuff on Michael's wrist.

Michael was struggling to put on his shirt. He had been cuffed while wearing it, and it had ended up twisted around the chain when they removed it in their frenzy to get close to each other. "Be careful, okay? Don't take any risks. I'd rather stay here indefinitely than know you were hurt because of me."

His expression was almost angry, but she knew it

was concern for her. It warmed her heart.

"I'll be careful, I promise. You too, okay? Don't do anything to raise their ire. I don't want you hurt again."

Michael stepped up to her and helped her off the cot to stand on her good leg. He pulled her into his arms and held her tightly to him for several seconds. After kissing the top of her head, he let her go and bent to retrieve her crutches from the floor.

CHAPTER 8

Michael lay down on his cot after Steph left him. His whole body was crying out for his mate. Letting her walk out that door and lock it between them had been torture, and he had to clamp his mouth shut to keep from telling her to come back. All he wanted was to keep her with him and make her his. But doing that would ensure both of their deaths, or something worse. Jack was capable of torture to exact his revenge. Michael had no doubt.

He breathed out a long breath and tried to calm both his body and mind. There had to be something he could do to help Steph get away from Jack. If she could get in touch with James, he might find a way to help her.

Michael swore under his breath. He should have given her James's phone number before she left, but he had forgotten about it. At one point he had been leading up to it, but she didn't want to listen to him. Steph had been clear that she wouldn't leave him there on his own. And then they had been so caught up in each other that he had hardly been able to remember his own name. The thought of her mewling and wriggling as he gave her pleasure entered his mind, and his rock-hard shaft started throbbing. He wanted her, but it was more than that. His body was in full mating mode, wanting to secure her as his as soon as possible. It would ease over time, he was sure, but the question was whether it would take an hour, a day, or even longer. He had no experience with that kind of thing.

Trying to clear his mind of his need, Michael started methodically going through everything he had seen and heard since meeting Jack and his brutes. But he didn't come up with anything that would be useful in his current situation.

He studied the cuff on his wrist for what must be the tenth time at least, but other than unlocking it with a key, he couldn't come up with a way to remove it. The cuff was a kind he had never seen before, but then he wasn't in the habit of restraining people. There was some sort of sleeve surrounding his wrist, and trying to move the cuff up or down his arm caused it to tighten. Even if he changed into his serval he would be stuck in the thing. They had really thought of everything to make sure their prisoners wouldn't be able to escape.

∞∞∞∞

Back in her room, Steph couldn't help the tears flowing down her cheeks. This was so fucked up. Finding a key for the cuff on Michael's wrist seemed like an impossible task. There was no way that was going to be just lying around somewhere for her to easily get her hands on. And cutting the cuff off? She had no idea where to find the tools to do it. Some type of bolt cutter might work, but it would be difficult to cut the snug-fitting cuff without cutting Michael as well.

Why couldn't she just have met Michael instead of Jack those months ago? It would have been perfect. Days of hiking in the Scottish Highlands and nights of fucking like bunnies in heat.

"Oh, snap out of it!" Steph berated herself for her stupid daydreaming and self-pity. "This won't get you anywhere."

She pulled in a deep breath and let it out slowly. It was time she got to work. She had to find a way to get Michael out of this place. Nobody would know where to look for him, so it was all up to her.

The key to the cuff had been used when Jack's goons put Michael in that cell. One of them either had the key on his person at the time or he picked it up on the way to the cell. However, it was likely that both of the assholes carried a key at all times. Those two brutes were Jack's main muscle and seemed to be responsible for handling the prisoners.

Stealing a key from one of them, however, would be damn near impossible the way Steph saw it. She could feign falling into one of their laps but knowing them, they wouldn't hesitate to throw her to the floor rather than catch her, and there would be no time to go through any of their pockets as part of that scenario.

From what she had observed in the time she had been at the estate, the goons had rooms above the garage. Searching their rooms might have been an option, if not for the fact that she wouldn't be able to get to the garage without being stopped. Steph had tried to get ahold of a vehicle several times in her previous escape attempts, resulting in there being a guard stationed outside the garage at all times to keep her away.

Back to the bolt cutter. The most likely place to find one of those was in the garage, which was a no-go. There might be a bolt cutter kept somewhere in the house, but if that was the case, she had no idea where.

Steph sighed in frustration and almost wished Michael hadn't shown up at the warehouse to find her. But if she was being honest with herself, the two hours they had spent together since he showed up out of the blue, was two hours she wouldn't want to be without. She would cherish the time they had together for the rest of her life, no matter what happened to her.

An idea suddenly popped into her head, and before she could check herself, she stood up. Only to wince and sit down again as pain shot up her broken leg. After she took a few deep breaths, the pain subsided a little, and she was able to think.

Steph didn't have a key to the cuff, but she did have access to needles. She had never picked a lock before in her life, but it must be possible. At least worth a try.

The urge to return to Michael immediately to test her idea was strong, but it was too late in the evening. Jack's guests would be leaving at any time if they hadn't already. And when they were gone, the usual nighttime patrolling of the house would start. Venturing out at night was risky business with a high possibility for detection, and she was expressly forbidden to move around outside her room at night. It would have to wait until morning.

∞∞∞∞

It was early morning when James opened the door and welcomed Trevor and Duncan into the hotel room. Carlos was already there. Ann and Marna had gone down to the breakfast restaurant at their hotel to pick up some food for them all. They would eat breakfast while planning.

James and the three other men had visited Jack's warehouse late the night before, but it had been deserted. Both James and Trevor had shifted to see if they could pick up Michael's scent. None of them had been close enough to Stephanie to recognize hers.

Michael had been inside the warehouse, and his scent was mixed with that of one human female and three male panther shifters. There were no signs of a struggle, but there was no doubt that Michael had been caught and most likely taken to the estate. A quick sniff around confirmed that Jack was involved in the drug trade, but no other useful information was found that would help them in their rescue of Michael and Stephanie.

Trevor and Duncan sat down on the couch and Trevor went straight to the point. "I've had my people working on finding out as much as possible about the security system, guard routines, layout of the house and estate grounds, and so on. But even using all their tricks, they've hardly been able to find anything. It's like the estate doesn't have any kind of electronic security system at all, which is unusual. The only thing my people have been able to find out is that Jack has hired a guard service company from time to time."

"I know a couple of panther shifters." Duncan let his gaze move between the other three males. "They're skittish and careful, never sharing anything about their clan. Seems like Jack's keeping a tight rein on his panthers and doesn't want anyone in his business, clan or otherwise."

"Sounds like we have no way of getting the information we need to plan this operation properly." James was worried, and with good reason too. "I don't like going in blind, when we know that the clan leader is a nasty piece of work with drug connections."

"What if we use a drone to scout the area?" Carlos was leaning forward in his seat. "If we can get ahold of one of those long-range silent models, military grade, if possible, I've got experience operating most of those."

"Good thinking." James grinned at Carlos before shifting his gaze to Trevor. "Any chance you know someone with that kind of toy? You seem to have connections."

Trevor chuckled and nodded. "That I have. I think I can get what you need. Just have to make a couple of calls."

There were excited voices in the corridor outside, and a few seconds later Ann, Marna, and Jennie came in with a trolley loaded with food and drinks.

They had barely closed the door behind them before Ann started telling them what the women were so excited about. "We overheard a couple of women talking downstairs in the restaurant. They're staying at the hotel because they're going to attend a mating ceremony tomorrow. Jack's mating ceremony."

All the men rose as one and the room seemed far more crowded all of a sudden.

James grabbed his wife's hand and stared at her. "Did they say anything more?"

"They were worried about what to wear since the invite specified formal wear, but the ceremony is going to take place outside, and the weather is unpredictable around here. And apparently there are people invited from all the panther clans in Scotland and some in England as well. There will be a lot of people attending."

Everyone started talking around them, but James grabbed his wife and planted a hard kiss on her mouth. "My woman. What would I do without you?"

Ann raised an eyebrow at him in challenge. "Keep that in mind the next time you try to leave me behind to make sure I'm safe. I have my uses."

"Oh, you most certainly do." James let a smidgen of the desire he was feeling for her fill his eyes. If they didn't have guests, he would throw her on the bed right at this moment and fuck her until she begged him to stop. And knowing Ann that would take a while.

Someone clearing their throat brought them out of their bubble and Ann laughed. "Later, babes." Then, she turned to the other people present in the room with them.

Jennie grinned at them before sliding her gaze to Trevor and blowing him a kiss.

James cleared his throat. "Well done, ladies. Sounds like we've got a party to crash tomorrow. We'll need suitable clothing and a plan for how to get in without raising suspicions. And of course, a plan for how to find Michael and Stephanie when we get there.

Hopefully the drone footage will help us make viable plans."

"And"—Marna cut him off—"the women we overheard mentioned leaving the hotel at one o'clock tomorrow, so I guess the ceremony starts around two in the afternoon."

James nodded in approval. "Perfect. Then we know when and where. We'll only have to work on the how. Let's do that over breakfast."

CHAPTER 9

Steph had just gotten out of the shower and dressed when there was a knock on her door. It was still quite early, so she was a bit surprised. Nobody usually bothered her until later in the day, if at all. She wasn't a part of clan life, and she had no intention of ever becoming a part of it either, so Steph kept to herself as much as possible.

For a few weeks after arriving at the estate the first time, she had actively sought Jack out and tried to force him to let her leave, usually by screaming and being in his face whenever he was working or having guests. But after suffering his fists a number of times, she'd changed her strategy. Staying in her room as much as possible, she had planned her escape. She only left her room for food or to gather information that might help her get out of there.

"I'm coming." She used her crutches to get to the door. Opening it, she stared up into Jack's face.

He glanced at what she was wearing and narrowed

his eyes at her. "Going somewhere?"

Steph sighed. She had used her loose-fitting shorts the night before, so her clothing options were reduced to one. A deep-blue dress with a plunging neckline. It was way too formal for everyday use, but with no other choice, she had put it on. "It's all I've got that will fit at the moment." She lifted her injured leg to support her explanation. "I'll do some laundry today, but I need a couple of loose-fitting pants to wear."

Jack's grin took her aback, and she was just getting ready to retreat into her room and close the door in his face when he spoke.

"That's easily solved. It's part of the reason I'm here actually. Come with me."

Jack's suddenly good mood had her reeling. It was never a good sign in her experience. Steph wanted to stay in her room, but she knew what would happen if she disobeyed a direct order.

They moved through the house with Jack leading the way and then ending up outside the door to his office on the ground floor. He turned to her like he wanted to say something, but then he seemed to change his mind and opened the door instead. Jack moved to the side and motioned for her to enter ahead of him, and Steph felt her apprehension rising. She had no idea what to expect.

On entering the room, she stopped as her eyes landed on a woman sitting in Jack's office chair. Swinging her gaze to Jack, Steph was surprised to see him smiling at the woman. She would have expected Jack to react with anger on seeing someone using his chair, but there was only delight, perhaps even a bit of awe, in his gaze. Steph felt her trepidation grow. This couldn't be good. Anyone eliciting that kind of reaction from Jack was someone to fear.

"Ah, so this is the famous Stephanie." The woman's husky voice drew Steph's eyes to her, almost like she had been issued an order to do so.

Steph didn't say anything, just gave a slight nod to acknowledge the woman's statement.

The woman rose from Jack's office chair and rounded his desk to approach Steph. "I'm Ambrosia. You may address me using my name."

Ambrosia was tall and beautiful with long red-gold hair and deep-green eyes. She was immaculately dressed in a long, flowing creation. The dress was in a green color that accentuated the color of her eyes and drew your gaze to them.

Steph found she didn't want to meet the other woman's gaze. There was something disturbing about the intensity in Ambrosia's eyes as well as the woman herself. Instead of saying anything, Steph nodded like before and kept her gaze on the woman's chin.

"You're an odd one, aren't you?" Ambrosia frowned at Steph before turning her attention to Jack. "Where did you find this one, Jack?"

Steph wanted to protest being talked about like she was a small child, but she refrained. Something told her it was better for her to keep her mouth shut as much as possible in the woman's presence.

"I followed your advice. She doesn't have any close family or friends that would miss her."

Steph couldn't help the shocked expression on her face as she stared at Jack. Thoughts and feelings tumbled through her like clothes in a dryer, and she had trouble focusing. Nothing made sense and she couldn't seem to catch one single thought, just a tangle of them.

A hand grabbing her arm painfully broke through the mess in her head, and she realized she had let go of her crutches and was tilting sideways. Jack had grabbed her arm to keep her from falling.

"I can see that you've kept her in the dark about why she's here." There was no emotion in Ambrosia's tone. "I guess we should get started."

Steph's head was clearing, and with it her shock was turning into fury. What did they mean she had no one that would miss her? Was that his only reason for choosing her to be his mate? Why? Not that his reason really mattered, but she would still like to know.

But before she could utter any of her many questions, Jack swept her up in his arms and deposited her on the couch.

"You fucking asshole." The pure hatred in her voice must have been obvious even to Jack, and he took a step back like she had pushed him. "I hate you, and I always will."

His face contorted with rage, and he took a step toward her. Undoubtedly to hit her like he usually did when she defied him or didn't conform to his plans.

But Steph wasn't scared. She was too furious to be afraid of him at the moment. Letting her expression show her anger, disgust, and defiance, she watched him closing the distance between them like he was in slow motion. He might as well kill her because she would rather be dead than be his mate.

Jack's movements suddenly froze, and a cold breeze tugged at Steph's braid. The sudden temperature drop had her shivering and moving her gaze around in search of the source of the gust of wind.

"Temper, Jack." Ambrosia's cool voice sent icy tendrils down Steph's spine. Cold sweat beaded on her forehead while she hugged herself to try to stay warm.

Ambrosia turned her gaze on Steph, and she frowned when she met the woman's cold pale-green stare. Just a minute ago, Ambrosia's eyes had been a deeper green color.

The woman moved her attention back to Jack and nodded at a chair. "Sit down, Jack."

A bit sluggishly, he did as she commanded. Then he shook his head a little, and a look of confusion moved over his face, but he stayed seated and didn't say anything.

Steph had no idea what had just happened. If she didn't know better, she would have said that Ambrosia had taken control over Jack's body and mind, forcing her will upon him. But that was just crazy. Then again it wasn't that long ago that Steph had found out about shifters being real. Wasn't it possible that other creatures from folklore existed as well, like witches?

"Now, let's get started." Ambrosia swung her gaze to Steph. "The first point on our agenda is to do something about your leg."

"It's broken. Not much I can do about that." Steph shrugged and kept her eyes on the woman's chin.

"But I can." Smiling, Ambrosia approached the couch.

Steph felt herself frowning. She wanted to keep her distance from the woman, but getting away when her crutches were halfway across the room was damn near impossible. And even with the crutches, she wasn't any match for people with two working legs.

"Don't worry." Ambrosia knelt in front of Steph. "This won't hurt a bit."

Watching as the woman's hands reached out toward her leg, Steph had to stop herself from moving away. A mixture of fear and revulsion raced through her, but she steeled herself for whatever was coming.

Ambrosia's hands were warm, which was a bit of a shock. Steph had expected them to be cold like the breeze earlier. A tingling feeling started beneath the woman's hands where she had placed them just above the cast at Steph's knee. Then heat spread down her leg, and the pain of her injury receded. Steph forgot to breath as she felt her own hands start tingling in response to the healing power being used to mend her leg. It was incredible how her own power rose up in answer to the power being used upon her body, and she felt a strong compulsion to let their powers meet and combine.

The woman kneeling in front of her jerked, and Ambrosia's eyes snapped to Steph's face.

Suddenly aware of what she had been allowing, Steph clamped down on her power and forced it to recede while trying to maintain the surprised expression on her face. There was no reason not to be surprised at what the woman was doing to her. Any normal person would be.

But Steph didn't want Ambrosia to know that she wasn't the only one in the room who was able to heal. Steph had a feeling that as a normal human, she was largely discounted as an asset. Showing anything other than normal behavior or abilities wouldn't count in Steph's favor. She would become more valuable to the panthers, and perhaps even to this woman, and consequently watched more closely. And most likely exploited as well.

"That feels incredible. The pain is gone." Steph tried to sound in awe of what she was experiencing, in an effort to distract Ambrosia from whatever the woman had felt when Steph's power had risen up.

Silence reigned for several seconds, and Steph focused on breathing normally while waiting for Ambrosia's reaction. One of two scenarios were most likely, none of them good. Either she would see Steph as a competitor or someone to be exploited. Steph only had one option. Act as though she had no idea what Ambrosia was talking about.

"I'm not just removing your pain. Your leg will be healed in a few minutes." Ambrosia's head tilted down as she moved her hands to Steph's foot and continued her healing from that end of the cast.

"Really?" Breathing out a silent sigh of relief, Steph hoped that Ambrosia had dismissed what she had felt as a bit strange but nothing worth investigating. Steph needed to be more careful in the future, knowing there were others with her abilities out there.

The next few minutes, Ambrosia kept pouring her power into Steph's leg, and there was no doubt her leg was healing. Jack's words to her earlier about her reduced clothing options being easily solved came back to her. He obviously knew what Ambrosia was capable of, but Steph had never seen the woman at the estate before. Not that Steph was privy to everything that was going on in the house, but the woman was no frequent guest.

She glanced over at Jack, who was still in the chair Ambrosia had ordered him to sit in. He seemed to be following what Ambrosia was doing to Steph's leg with a bit of an odd expression on his face. Like he was in a trance but still able to notice some of what was going on around him. Studying him more closely, she saw something that made her shudder and quickly look away from him. Jack was fully aroused.

The sight was disgusting to Steph, but it made her remember something. Michael had become aroused after she healed him. Steph had thought that was because she was touching his delicate parts, but that might not have been the reason. Or at least not the only reason. Thinking back, her ex-boyfriend had become aroused as well when she healed his hand. She had never considered it before, but perhaps her power had something to do with the resulting arousal. And consequently, if Jack was aroused, it might be as a result of Ambrosia using her power on him. Not her healing power, but in Jack's case some sort of commanding or persuasive power.

"Now we cut off the cast."

Steph started when Ambrosia broke the silence.

The woman rose from her kneeling position in front of Steph and walked to Jack's desk. Coming back with a heavy duty bolt cutter in her hands, she settled in front of Steph.

Steph stared at the bolt cutter in Ambrosia's hands. It was just what she needed to cut off the cuff on Michael's wrist, or judging from the size of the tool, perhaps cutting the chain would be better.

"Don't worry. I won't cut you."

Ambrosia must have misinterpreted Steph's expression as one of fear as she stared at the large tool. If she had known what Steph had been thinking, the woman wouldn't have been impressed. It was evident from Jack and Ambrosia's earlier exchange that the woman had been giving him advice on who to choose as a mate. The big question Steph was left with was why. Jack was a handsome man, and there were plenty of single women in his own clan who wanted to mate him. So why didn't he choose one of them instead of Steph? Not counting the day before, she had never made a secret of despising him. And choosing to mate someone who hated you was a strange thing to do. There was something that didn't add up about this situation, and Steph would bet big money on it having something to do with Ambrosia and whatever powers she had.

The cast fell away from Steph's leg as the woman finished cutting. Ambrosia put the bolt cutter down on the floor beside her and indicated for Steph to get up.

Carefully rotating her ankle, Steph smiled. There was no pain, and her leg seemed fully healed. Standing up was no problem, and she took a turn around the room to fully test her leg before ending up standing in front of Ambrosia.

"Thank you, Ambrosia." Steph meant it. The healing of her leg was carried out to make sure the mating ceremony would go ahead as planned, but Steph didn't care about that. The main benefit of having two fully functional legs again was that it significantly increased her and Michael's chances of escape. And if she could get ahold of that bolt cutter, the odds might tip in their favor.

There was something Steph would like to know, though. "Can we speak privately for a few minutes?" She quickly glanced at Jack, but there was no reaction to her question. "I've got a few questions I'd like to ask you, if that's okay with you?"

Ambrosia narrowed her eyes and let the silence reign for several seconds before she answered. "We can speak here. Jack is, shall we say, on a break. But first let me deal with this." The woman was looking at her cheek.

Steph nodded, realizing that the woman meant the bruise on her cheek. Ambrosia's hand touched her cheek lightly and stayed only a minute before the woman let her hand fall to her side and took a step back.

"Okay, you can ask your questions."

Steph cleared her mind of all emotions, or at least she tried as best she could. She would only be able to talk about this if she pretended it had nothing to do with her personally.

"Is there a particular reason Jack has chosen me to be his mate?"

There was a look of surprise on Ambrosia's face. "There's no anger in you at the moment. I thought you hated him for that." The woman paused a couple of seconds before she continued. "Jack needs to mate a human. Someone strong who can handle the transformation the mating will bring."

Fear tried to choke her at Ambrosia's words, but Steph forced it out of her mind and continued. She needed to know more, no matter what happened from this point onward. "What do you mean by transformation?"

Amusement seemed to play on Ambrosia's lips. "Jack wants to rule the panthers. Not just as alpha of this clan, but as king of all the panthers. And I've found a way to make that happen. With a little help, the power of the mating bond will fuel a transformation in him that will bring his alpha power to a higher level. A significantly higher level."

Steph could feel herself frowning. "But wouldn't mating a female panther increase the strength of the mating bond?"

"Yes, it would. But it would be difficult to limit the transformation to Jack alone." Ambrosia raised an eyebrow at Steph like she was issuing a challenge.

It didn't take Steph many seconds to realize what the woman meant. "He needs to mate a human. Otherwise he might end up sharing his throne with an equally powerful queen."

"Exactly. Jack wants to rule alone and mating a human will ensure that. But the human has to survive the transformation and stay healthy, since the power of the mating bond is dependent on the existence of a mate."

She shouldn't be surprised. Jack was an egotistical power-hungry bastard. Steph knew that already. She had a few more questions, though, before she could go back to her room and have a well-deserved meltdown.

"I assume you're a witch." She kept her eyes on Ambrosia's face to judge her reaction to this, but there was none that she could see. "What's in it for you?"

The woman's burst of laughter made Steph take a step back. There was something dark and evil in that laughter.

"Oh, I think I'll keep most of the details to myself. Let's just say there will be some benefits for me as well from this mating."

Fear was trying to take over her body, and Steph

felt an overwhelming need to get away from the witch. She had a bad feeling that the benefits the woman had just mentioned were going to have consequences for humanity and shifters alike. It wasn't just about the witch wanting longer life or more wealth. There was something more at play.

Steph swallowed down her fear. "Thank you for answering my questions."

She turned and walked away from Ambrosia, making sure not to hurry too much. It was better to give an impression of being cool and collected, instead of demonstrating her terror. Steph hated Jack and feared his fists, but those feelings were nothing compared to the dread she felt in the presence of Ambrosia.

CHAPTER 10

Somehow Michael had been able to sleep most of the night. He had no idea how, since he had been so focused on Steph, his whole body on fire with need and worry. But at some stage he had fallen asleep, possibly due to exhaustion. Or his body had simply decided to shut down after the most lifechanging day of his life.

The same petite woman who had brought him food the day before had come again the morning. He had tried asking her a couple of polite questions, like her name, but she had only shaken her head and left. Her manner spoke of a deep-seated anxiety, and he could only imagine what was the cause of that.

Nobody else had come to his room to check on him. He obviously wasn't a big concern to the panthers, or perhaps they were just that confident that he wouldn't be able to escape. Then again, the woman bringing him food probably reported back to them. And seeing as he was still cuffed and had treated her politely, there was no reason to consider him a threat.

And then there was their alpha's mating and all the preparations required for that. Jack was the type of person to use every opportunity to show himself off, and that would be the perfect occasion for him to do so.

Michael felt his muscles straining and his body preparing to change, but he had to suppress the urge. He had to keep believing that an opportunity for escape might still present itself and that he would be able to take Steph away from the estate. Anything else was too horrible to imagine.

The sound of light footsteps in the corridor had him sitting up and adopting a non-threating, relaxed pose. The door swung open, and time seemed to freeze as he stared into Steph's beautiful hazel eyes.

Before he could snap out of the thrill and shock of seeing her in his cell in the middle of the day, she had locked the door behind her and turned around to stand in front of him.

"Michael, are you all right?" There was worry in her eyes.

He mentally shook himself before grinning and reaching for her. Then she was in his arms, and he breathed a sigh of pure happiness at having her so close. His mate. It sang through him.

Loosening his hold on her, he looked into her eyes, and the happiness he saw there reflected his own.

"Kiss me already!" She breathed out the command in a low voice.

Michael didn't hesitate in crushing his lips to hers in a bruising kiss that reflected all his love for her. Yes, love. He loved this woman with all that he was. Even after knowing her for such a short time.

Their tongues tangled in a wicked dance of delight and promises of pleasure. Nothing and nobody else mattered but the two of them.

Steph moaned into his mouth, and the sound went straight to his cock, which hardened up so fast it felt like the blood flow to his brain stopped for a second. All he could focus on was the feel of his mate in his arms.

Changing her position, Steph ended up straddling him, and he felt her hot core pressing against his rock-hard shaft. Groaning he rubbed against her, imagining what it would feel like to push into her tight, wet pussy. Need like he had never felt before pounded through his body, and he sucked in a breath at the powerful feeling, effectively breaking their kiss.

"Steph, we have to stop, or I won't be able to." Michael stared into her eyes, and the desire reflected in them almost had him coming in his pants.

"I want you to make me yours. Your mate."

Michael's whole body resonated at her words, and it was like his heartbeat shouted, *Yes, Yes, Yes* in response to her request. But he quickly quelled his happiness. He suspected that the reason she wanted to be his mate was to prevent Jack from mating her. And although he fully understood her motive, and he would like nothing better than to be able to claim her as his, Michael couldn't do it. When they mated, it was going to be because she loved him and wanted to be his forever. But the main reason he couldn't mate her immediately was that it would be their death sentence. Jack would kill them. And before that he would take his time torturing them as revenge for destroying his plans and injuring his status.

Michael stared into her eyes, letting Steph see all his love for her. "I'd like nothing better, Steph, but I can't. Jack would kill us. Slowly and horribly. Trust me on that."

Her body deflated, and she leaned her forehead against his shoulder. "I know. I'm sorry. Forget I asked. It was selfish of me."

"No, no. Don't be sorry. I understand, and I would do it if I thought it would save you from Jack." And he realized he would, even if she could never love him the way he loved her. He would mate her to save her from the plans Jack had for her.

Steph lifted her head to stare into his eyes, tears welling in hers. "I should've met you earlier. Before Jack walked into my life and I made the stupidest mistake of my life. You're the most amazing man I've ever met, and I think I might be falling in love with you. Even though we've just met, and we hardly know each other. You probably think I'm crazy, but I mean it when I say that I've never felt like this before with anyone."

Michael was speechless, and for a few moments he allowed himself to wallow in the pure happiness her words brought him. It was so much more than he had hoped for. He already knew that Steph was attracted to him, but that she thought she was falling in love with him was so much better than that.

"I don't think you're crazy, Steph." He gave her a wide grin. "Because if you are, then so am I. I love you."

Michael watched as a series of emotions played across her face. From anxiety at having told him of her feelings to disbelief as he told her he loved her, and finally to a huge smile of joy when she understood that he meant what he had said.

"You love me?" Steph's voice was a whisper.

He nodded.

And then they were kissing again. Steph crushed her lips to his, and her arms wrapped around his neck. And Michael was helpless to do anything but respond. The feel of her body against his and her passionate kisses were making him lose all control. All he could think about was claiming her as his.

Her hands were moving down his chest and stomach, slowly caressing him through his shirt. Reaching his waist, her fingers found the button of his jeans and snapped it open, before slowly pulling down the zipper and freeing his cock.

The feel of her hands on him was heaven, and he rocked his hips as she closed one hand around his girth and started moving her hand up and down his length.

But the thought of what would happen to her if he came on her skin made him put his hand on hers to stop her movements.

"We have to stop." Michael used his other hand to cup her cheek as they stared at each other. "I'd like nothing better than to keep going, but I won't put you at risk of being hurt."

A small smile forming on Steph's lips had him frowning. Then she reached into her bra and pulled out a small package. She tore it open, and her smile widened. "I've got this."

The condom in her hand had Michael's cock twitch like it was doing a happy dance. "Steph." The gravel in his voice made him stop and clear his throat. "There's still a chance that—"

"Michael." She cut him off and stared at him with an expression of determination on her face. "This might be our only chance to be together, and unless you don't want me, I don't want to waste the short time we have. Will you fuck me or not?"

"No." He watched as her face fell. "But I'll make love to you."

The happy smile lighting up her face made him smile back.

Michael let his gaze travel down her body. He put his hands on her thighs to push the skirt of her dress up, when he suddenly stopped and stared. "Where is your cast?"

"Gone. My leg is healed."

He snapped his eyes up to hers before studying her face. "And your cheek. It's not just makeup covering the bruise, is it? But I thought you said—"

"Later. I'll explain everything later. Now I want you to make love to me."

He nodded and let his gaze drop to her lap. Pushing the material of her dress up to her hips, Michael stared at the junction of her thighs. Her pussy was covered by her panties, but he pushed his thumbs beneath the thin fabric and found her clit. Steph moaned and her jaw slackened. Gently caressing her small nub with his right thumb, he used his other thumb to play along her slit. Her female juices seeped out of her and soon coated both his fingers.

"Michael." Her voice was breathy, and she squirmed on his lap. "I want you inside me."

"Soon, beautiful. Very soon." He wanted to prepare

her body properly first. She was tight and, as she had pointed out the day before, he was big. He wanted to make sure she could take him without any discomfort. Her pleasure was essential.

***

Michael suddenly put his hands under her ass and rose before gently laying her down on her back on the cot. He pulled her panties down and stared at her down there. The heat in his eyes felt hot on her skin, and her clit started throbbing in response to his attention.

Throwing her panties on the floor, he leaned in between her legs while giving her a wicked grin. He licked up her slit before flicking his tongue over her pleasure button.

Steph almost cried out at the amazing feeling, but she managed to stop herself in time. Clamping her lips together, she stared down at Michael as he really went to town on her sensitive bits.

He alternated between sucking on her clit and circling it with his tongue, and she could feel the impending pleasure building like a ball of heat gathering in her lower abdomen.

"Michael, please. I need you inside me." Her voice was husky.

A finger entering her channel made her gasp. Then a second digit followed and started moving slowly in and out while rubbing her sensitive front wall.

Steph panted and moaned as Michael started vibrating his tongue over her clit. He increased the pace of his fingers inside her, and she suddenly tipped over the edge. Pleasure rolled through her, and she tried to close her thighs at the powerful sensations. But

Michael wouldn't let her and kept vibrating his tongue and moving his fingers to prolong her pleasure. When she came down, she was gasping for breath.

Opening her eyes, she watched as Michael rolled the condom down his impressive length. Thank the stars she had kept the large condoms she had brought with her to the estate several months ago. She had intended to throw them away weeks ago, but then she forgot.

Michael sat down on the cot. "Steph, I want you to ride me. That way you'll be in control and can take your time to let your body adjust to my size."

She nodded. He was huge, and she still wondered if he would fit inside her. He had said he would, though.

Steph straddled his thighs. She looked at Michael, and he grinned at her before she leaned forward and kissed him. Then she grabbed the hem of her dress and pulled it over her head.

Moving into position, she guided his cock to her entrance. The bulbous head was stretching her wider than she had ever been stretched before as she slowly lowered her body. Panting, she moved her body up and down several times, his shaft penetrating her a little deeper each time until he was finally buried to the hilt.

Michael sucked in a breath, and she opened her eyes and stared into his. The pinched look on his face had her frowning.

"Are you okay?"

Michael nodded slowly before clearing his throat. "Just stay there and don't move for a little while. You're so tight, and you feel so good. I don't want this to be over too soon."

Steph smiled in satisfaction. She was doing this to him, and she liked the thought of that.

He leaned forward and kissed her slowly. She opened her mouth, and the intensity of the kiss increased.

Michael's hands on her hips lifted her slowly, and she let him guide her pace as she started moving up and down, shuddering in pleasure at the feel of his thick cock filling her to capacity.

The ball of heat in her lower abdomen was back and building fast as his shaft rubbed places inside of her that had hardly been touched before. She increased the pace and force of her movements, and suddenly she landed on her back on the cot.

***

Michael drove into her tight, wet channel in long hard thrusts. His muscles were straining with the need to come, but he wouldn't spill before he had given Steph another orgasm.

Her channel walls started fluttering, and his thrusts became more erratic as her walls clamped down around his cock. His orgasm detonated through his system, the shock waves taking his breath away as he rocked into Steph's tight sheath, trying to prolong her orgasm. When he finally came down, he blinked his eyes open and stared at the most beautiful sight he had ever seen.

Steph gazed up at him with hooded eyes and a satisfied smile on her face, her hair spread around her head in a chestnut-colored halo. The sight had his heart squeeze painfully in dread of what was supposed to happen in the morning.

He quickly looked down to prevent her from seeing

the expression of pain and sorrow on his face. "I have to get rid of this." Michael gently pulled out of her and went to the toilet. After flushing down the evidence of their lovemaking and cleaning himself thoroughly, he turned around to find Steph fully dressed and sitting on the cot.

She sighed. "I need to tell you something."

Michael picked up his jeans and started to put them on. "About your leg?"

"Yes, that's part of it." She paused and swallowed. "Jack came to my room this morning."

He felt his muscles bunch, and something must have shown on his face.

"No, he didn't hurt me, just asked me to follow him. There was a woman in his office." Steph paused again, a look of horror on her face.

Michael sat down beside her and took her hand. "Did she hurt you?"

She shook her head and continued. "No, she healed my leg and my cheek."

"But that's a good thing, isn't it?" Something didn't add up. Fear was emanating from her even as she told him that the woman had healed her.

"Yes, but that's not the only thing this woman, Ambrosia, can do. She's a witch, Michael, and she's the one who encouraged Jack to find a human to mate."

Michael felt himself frowning. He had heard rumors of people who always seemed to be able to manipulate situations to their advantage, but he had never believed it to be anything other than good old-fashioned persuasion technique. Perhaps he had to reconsider his perception of several things in the world.

"What did she do to make you say that she's a witch?"

"She forced her will upon Jack. It was strange. He was about to hit me, but she told him to sit down in a chair. There was this gust of cold wind as she gave him the command. And then he obeyed. He just sat down, looking like he was in some sort of trance, and he was still like that when I left the office."

Michael stared at Steph. "Do you know if she did something similar to you while you were with her?"

Steph shook her head. "No. Well, it's difficult to be completely sure since I don't know what she might be capable of, but I don't think so. She healed my leg the same way I healed you. In fact, her healing power felt so similar to my own that my power tried to rise up as well, but I think I managed to force it down in time. She noticed something, but I don't think she realized what it was. At least she didn't act like she did or ask me any questions about it."

Breathing out a sigh of relief, Michael smiled at her. He could understand that the experience had frightened Steph, and that she felt uncomfortable around the woman, but everything seemed to have worked out well. Jack was neutralized and Steph's leg was healed. It sounded like Michael actually owed Ambrosia his gratitude for taking care of Steph.

"Sounds like everything worked out fine."

Shaking her head, Steph gripped his hand firmly. "Ambrosia is dangerous. She can manipulate people. But what really scares me is what she's planning."

He felt his smile drain away. "Tell me."

"The witch is going to turn Jack into a king. Using the power of our mating bond, she's going to increase his alpha power significantly and turn him into the king of the panthers."

Michael's spine turned to ice, and he felt himself go pale.

"She specifically encouraged him to find a human mate to avoid having to share his power with a panther queen. And she's not doing this for Jack's benefit. This is about her and what she will gain from it. I just don't know what that is. She wouldn't tell me. But it must be something special for her to allow someone like Jack to gain that kind of power. If Ambrosia didn't think she would be the one getting the most out of this, she wouldn't do it."

"Fuck." Michael was reeling. For him the worst consequence of the mating would always be to lose Steph, but for the world that was nothing compared to the other ramifications. It would completely change the power structure for the panthers, and if Ambrosia could pull that off, what would happen next? Would she go after the wolves, the bears, the servals? The whole supernatural world might be changed, and not for the better. And the humans? No doubt they would be affected too.

"Steph." He held onto her hand and stared into her eyes, willing her to heed his words. "You have to escape. For yourself, and for the rest of the world. Forget about me. I don't matter in this. Find my friend James. He'll know what to do."

She was already shaking her head with an angry expression on her face by the time he stopped talking. "No, I won't leave you here with them."

"Please, Steph. It's the only way. I can't get out of here, see?" He rattled the chain connecting the cuff on his wrist to the wall.

Tears welled in her eyes, and Michael let go of her hand to cup her cheeks. "Go, Steph. With all the planning and preparations for what I assume is going to be a grand mating ceremony, you might be able to get away. Just be careful."

"No, Michael. You're coming with me. I'm going to find a bolt cutter and cut that chain. Then we'll go."

The defiance in her eyes made him groan in defeat. He would never be able to stand up to this woman. She had him firmly on a leash. The thing was, he didn't mind that so much, apart from this moment when he wanted her to focus on her own safety.

Steph put her hands on his chest. "I'll be back as soon as I can get ahold of that bolt cutter. Ambrosia used it to cut off my cast. It was in Jack's office earlier. I just couldn't grab it while she was watching."

He leaned forward and brushed his lips over hers in a gentle kiss before pulling back and staring into her eyes. "Be careful."

Nodding, she rose from the cot.

"I can't hear anyone approaching." Michael nodded at the door, indicating the corridor.

She carefully unlocked the door and took a peek into the corridor. Then Steph disappeared through the door, and he was left alone in his cell with a sinking feeling in his stomach. This was bad, and he had a horrible feeling that it was only going to get worse.

CHAPTER 11

James and Carlos were in a small clearing not far from the fence surrounding the estate. With the help of Duncan, they had found a spot just behind a small rise, preventing them from being seen by anyone patrolling inside the fence. The distance to the estate house itself was about six hundred yards, well within the range of the powerful drone Trevor had been able to get ahold of on short notice. Proving again that the wolf had some powerful connections.

"Anything I can do?" James whispered and shot a glance at Carlos before returning his attention to their surroundings. Duncan had shifted to his wolf and was patrolling the area around them. He would bark three times if anyone approached to give them time to hide their equipment. There were hiking trails not too far away, so the two of them walking through the forest shouldn't raise any suspicions, but the drone equipment would.

"Nah, I've got this." Carlos continued setting up

the drone for flight and checking the controls and cameras. Most people took his quiet demeanor to mean he wasn't particularly bright and clever, but Carlos was a genius when it came to operating any kind of gadget. Or repairing them, for that matter.

Another minute and the drone was ready for flight. James stood back a little, but the drone eased graciously into the air and hugged the trees as it moved silently away from them.

Carlos was staring at the drone controller in his hands, carefully maneuvering the drone based on the various camera images. "I'll stay close to the trees to avoid detection. The camouflage color of the drone should keep it well hidden."

James kept his eyes and ears on their surroundings while Carlos worked in silence. When his friend swore, James was at his side in a heartbeat. "What happened? Did you crash?"

"No." Carlos stared at the camera images. "That fucking asshole."

Looking at his friend's face, James frowned. Carlos was seriously pissed off, and that didn't happen very often. "Then what?"

"This Jack character deserves whatever nasty we can send at him. His mating ceremony is going to be according to the ancient traditions. I can't imagine any modern female agreeing to this."

James stared at Carlos. "As in tying the female up for all to watch as they mate?" It was barbaric. From a time when females were property and traded like sheep. They didn't usually get a choice of whom to mate. That was decided by the alpha. Thankfully, that old tradition had been discarded several centuries ago, or at least that was what he had thought.

"Yes, it's fucking disgusting. Who would want to watch something like that? I sure as hell wouldn't."

James swore. "I guess that's another reason we need to attend the mating ceremony tomorrow. If the female Jack's going to mate hasn't been given a choice, we need to do everything we can to help her."

∞∞∞∞

They all gathered in the hotel room again in the afternoon to finalize their plans for the next day. Carlos had just shown some of the drone footage on the TV and presented his sketches of the estate grounds based on what he had been able to see. The stage and setup for the mating ceremony were still visible on the TV screen.

"Do you really think Jack will go through with something like that?" Ann was staring at the screen in disbelief. "People will object, won't they?" She moved her gaze around the room.

James squeezed her hand and looked at all the shocked faces in the room. At least it didn't seem like the old tradition was any more alive in Scotland than it was in America. Trevor and Duncan seemed just as horrified as the rest of them. Not that he had expected otherwise, but it was good to get it confirmed.

Jennie nodded. "I wonder if any of their guests from the other clans know about this or if it's going to be a surprise. I can't imagine the women we overheard down in the restaurant this morning would approve. Tell me if you don't agree, but they didn't seem like the kind of women who would go along with something like that."

Marna and Ann both nodded.

"I agree." Ann kept her eyes on Jennie. "And if that's correct, there will be a lot of shocked people at the mating ceremony tomorrow. I say we start spreading the word about what's going to take place there as soon as we get inside the gate. The more people we can rile up about the pending atrocities the better."

Trevor laughed. "That might actually work. Nothing like an angry crowd to fuck up the asshole's barbaric plans, and a great distraction to help hide our search-and-rescue mission."

"And I've got us all tickets to the show. Or more accurately, we won't need tickets." Duncan grinned. "Turns out I know one of the guys working for the guard service company Jack has been using from time to time. They're going to work the gate tomorrow, but they're not allowed on the estate grounds. He has promised to let us in without an invitation in return for me putting in a good word for him with a woman he likes."

James smiled and let his gaze glide over the people in the room with him. He felt his worry about their party-crashing decrease a little. This could work. They were a good team, and hopefully in twenty-four hours Michael and Stephanie would be out of Jack's hands and hidden somewhere safe.

"And clothes?" James looked at his wife. "Did you find something for us to wear tomorrow?" The women had been out shopping with Trevor as their guide and bodyguard, while James, Carlos, and Duncan had been filming at the estate.

Ann turned to him with a wide grin. "Oh, yes, you're going to be trying it on later. I can't wait." The hint of desire in her eyes had him wishing everyone would leave their room. Fast.

"Okay." He wrenched his gaze away from his beautiful wife to address the room. "Thank you so much, all of you, for helping us find Michael and Stephanie." He nodded at Trevor and Duncan. "Without you I don't think we would've stood much of a chance of getting Michael back, or rescuing Stephanie from whatever she's mixed up with. Of course, we haven't yet confirmed that they're at the estate and okay, but I now feel confident that we will find them. And it's all thanks to you. Without your quick thinking and connections, we wouldn't even know where to look. We'll owe you for this. Anytime you need help, just tell us and we'll be there."

"Thank you, James, but you don't owe us anything." Trevor shot his mate, Jennie, a look filled with love and awe. "Without you I wouldn't have found my mate. So, really, this is just a small down payment toward what I owe you."

James laughed. "Okay, let's call it even then."

"Deal." Trevor grinned and got up from the couch where he had been sitting with Jennie and Duncan. "I think we'll leave you to try on your party clothes." He winked at Ann before grabbing Jennie's hand and pulling her along with him toward the door. "Perhaps we need to do that as well."

"Couples." Duncan sighed and feigned an irritated look before chuckling. "Have fun you lot. This single man will go read a book or something." Following behind Trevor and Jennie, he disappeared out the door.

"See you at dinner?" Carlos had his arm around Marna's waist as they walked toward the door.

"Yes, we'll be there." James nodded.

Marna squealed when Carlos's hand slipped down and grabbed a handful of her ass as they disappeared through the door.

"Hmm, I wonder what everyone's going to be doing for the next couple of hours." James had intended to sound serious, but he couldn't help the amusement in his voice. He checked the door to make sure it was locked and turned back to Ann.

His focus dropped to her chest. In the few seconds he'd had his back to her she had discarded her top. Wearing only her bra and a miniskirt, she was sitting on the bed with her legs apart and leaning back on her arms. James felt his mouth go dry at the sight.

"I don't think you'll have time to wonder about that." Ann's smile was teasing. "You'll be trying on clothes remember? Pants, jacket, shirt, bowtie. I think perhaps in that order."

"What?"

"Yes, you have to try on each piece individually and walk around so I can see how it fits from all angles." Ann chuckled and lifted the hem of her skirt for a second before letting it fall back to rest between her thighs.

James groaned. His cock was as hard as steel already, and the sight of her pink pussy didn't exactly help. Somehow, she had managed to remove her panties as well while he had been focused on the door. And she was going to make him parade around for her, when all he wanted to do was lift her skirt and push into her wet heaven. But two could play at that game.

He took his time opening each button of his shirt before slowly taking it off. Then, he snapped open the button on his jeans before stopping and looking at his wife. Her mouth was half open while she was staring at his crotch. Palming his hard cock through his jeans, he groaned, and Ann's eyes snapped to his.

"James." She narrowed her eyes at him.

"Yes, dear." He inwardly cheered. It wouldn't be long before she gave up her teasing and launched herself at him. And he couldn't wait.

CHAPTER 12

Steph tried to stay out of the way of everyone who was preparing for the mating ceremony. It seemed like the whole clan was present and busy, and the constant reminder of what was going to happen was threatening to throw her into a state of panic. With the amount of people around, it would be difficult to escape, even if she managed to get ahold of the bolt cutter to cut Michael's chain.

Jack seemed to be back to his normal self, and he had spent most of the day in his office with Ambrosia. Steph had been hovering around the area out of sight, hoping for an opportunity to get in and grab the bolt cutter. Assuming it was still there.

The office door opened, and Jack emerged. Ambrosia followed, and together they moved down the corridor and turned the corner at the end. Casually walking down the corridor and looking around the corner, Steph followed the pair with her eyes as they crossed the entrance hall and disappeared out the front door.

Steph turned and ran silently down the corridor and into Jack's office. She was in luck. The bolt cutter was still lying on the floor by the couch where Ambrosia had left it. Quickly, she grabbed the tool and returned to the office door. After checking that the corridor was empty, she exited Jack's office and walked a few yards down the corridor to a storage room. Closing the door behind her, she breathed a sigh of relief.

Okay. She had obtained the bolt cutter, step one on her list. It was time for step two, which was to bring the tool to Michael. Carrying it through the house for everyone to see wasn't an option, but she had found a way. Grabbing the role of packing tape she had put on the shelf earlier, she lifted the skirt of her dress and got to work. A few minutes later she had taped the bolt cutter to her inner thigh. It was going to be a bitch removing that tape, but that was nothing if she could free Michael.

Moving through the house was both nerve-racking and uncomfortable. Steph expected someone to come up to her at any time and lift her skirt. She tried to walk as naturally as she could, but her gait still felt a bit stilted. After taking a detour to her room, she continued down the hallway and used the back stairs down to the ground floor. The corridor outside the prison cells was empty, and after waiting a couple of minutes by the back stairs just to be sure, Steph hurried to Michael's cell and unlocked the door.

Michael smiled when she entered his cell, but it didn't quite reach his eyes. He seemed to be as worried as she was. She quickly locked the door and turned to him.

"Steph." He rose from the cot and reached out for her.

After taking two steps to reach him, she rose up on her toes and gave him a quick kiss.

"I've got a surprise for you." Stepping back and lifting her skirt, she smiled as his eyes widened in surprise.

He chuckled. "Looking under a woman's skirt is getting more and more interesting."

She smiled. "I might need some help removing the tape. It's kind of heavy-duty stuff."

Wincing, he lifted his gaze to hers. "That's going to hurt."

"I know, but I think the bolt cutter might be big enough to cut the chain, if not the cuff itself."

Michael nodded. "I think you're right, but what worries me is getting out of this place without getting caught. I don't want you getting hurt, and you will be if they catch us."

"So will you, Michael, and I don't want you getting hurt either. But it's our only chance. Nobody knows where we are. It's up to us to save ourselves."

He sighed. "I know." Then he squatted in front of her and raised his gaze to hers. "I'll be as careful as I can."

Michael started peeling away the tape from her thigh and Steph sucked in a breath at the pain. Even with him being careful, it still felt like her skin was being removed with the tape.

Finally, the tape was gone, and Michael rose with the bolt cutter in his hand. "Thank you for enduring that for me."

"You're welcome." She smiled up at him.

"But before we cut my chain, we need to come up with a plan for how to get out of here." He sat down on the cot and looked up at her. His expression appeared both serious and sad. It was obvious he had his doubts about their chances at escape.

Steph nodded and moved to him. Sitting down across his lap, she smiled at him, trying to convey all her love for him in that smile. It was still a bit staggering, the power of the feelings she had for Michael, but it felt so right, like it was meant to be somehow. She had never felt anything even remotely close to this for any other man, and she was willing to risk being caught for a chance at a future with this man.

Michael's serious expression broke into a smile, reaching his eyes this time. And the love shining back at her almost felt like heat on her skin. She would have been content staying like this for a long time. No kissing or making love, just staying in each other's presence with love radiating between them. Steph finally understood the saying "Love conquers all." Because who wouldn't do anything in their power to have this?

"I've been thinking about how to escape today while waiting to get into Jack's office. The wrought iron fence around this property is made of thick bars, and it's tall and hard to climb. Over the last few months, I've checked several sections of it. Last time I managed to escape using a tree that was close to the fence, but I'm sure they traced my scent there and have removed that tree by now."

Michael frowned and was about to say something, but she kept going to get to the point of her plan.

"But there's one section of the fence that's different. A short section of chain link fencing by a stream. It's tall, but we can cut through it with the bolt cutter. There's a drop of about fifteen feet right outside the fence, but I can climb down. I guess you can jump."

Narrowing his eyes in thought, Michael was silent for several seconds. Then he nodded slowly. "That could work. How far away is it?"

"About half a mile from the house, and the terrain is quite uneven with a lot of vegetation. It's easy to stay hidden as soon as we get more than a hundred yards away from the house. If we go now while they're all busy preparing for tomorrow, I think we can get away quite easily."

"Steph." Frowning in a way she was coming to know as his worried face, he stared at her. "If we do this I want to go first, alone."

She started to protest, but he cut her off.

"No, listen to me. I'll cross the exposed area close to the house and wait for you among the trees. You wait a couple of minutes to make sure nobody reacts to my movements before you follow. Then we can continue together. If they catch me while we're apart, you get back into the house and pretend not to know what has happened. That way they'll have no reason to hurt you. I'll be punished for trying to escape but not for helping you escape. We'll both be better off that way."

Steph sighed. He was right. "Okay."

Michael nodded. "Good. But are you sure it's going to be easier getting away unseen now rather than tonight?"

"Yes, there are always more people patrolling the grounds at night than during the day, and some will be in their panther form. I guess they don't expect people to try anything during the day, and that includes me. Last time I escaped it was just before dawn when the nighttime guards were getting tired and less focused. At least that was my theory, and it worked. They won't expect us to try to escape during broad daylight."

"Okay." He leaned forward and captured her lips in a searing kiss before he pulled back. "Then let me see what I can do about this chain."

Steph stood and let Michael move around to position the bolt cutter around the chain. With the thickness of the chain, she wasn't going to be a lot of help in cutting it. She simply wasn't strong enough.

Michael ended up having to cut through each side of a single chain link at a time not to break the bolt cutter. The cuff was still on his arm with a few links of chain attached to it, but at least he was no longer attached to the wall. He tore a strip of fabric from the material covering the mattress and tied it around the cuff and chain links still on his arm. It would prevent them from clinking as he moved.

Steph took his hands and stared up into his face. "I love you, Michael. No matter what happens, please remember that. And you have to promise me one thing. If they catch me, run. Please get out of here and get help. Giving yourself up won't save either of us. If you get away, we both have a chance."

His jaw tensed, and she could see that he wanted to say no. But there was sense in her words and that won out.

"Okay, but only if you promise the same. Don't

look back if they catch me. Get out of here and call James."

Steph agreed, and Michael repeated James's cell phone number several times until she had it memorized.

They would probably never be ready for the risk of capture and punishment, but it was time. After listening at the door for about a minute, Michael gave her the all-clear. Steph unlocked the door, and they carefully moved into the corridor. Leading the way, she headed for the exit located by the back stairs. It could be unlocked from the inside without a key and led to a section of the grounds rarely used.

She rounded the corner at the end of the corridor by the back stairs and immediately froze.

Ambrosia's green eyes narrowed as she stared past Steph at Michael behind her. "Stop."

The cold breeze made Steph shiver, and goosebumps broke out all over her body. She knew what she would see if she turned around. Michael would be standing there frozen, not able to take in what was going on around him.

"Please don't hurt him." She stared at Ambrosia, willing the woman to listen to her.

Moving her gaze to Steph, Ambrosia stared at her with anger tensing her features. "Why?"

There was only one thing she could say, and Steph felt her heart starting to break as she uttered the words. "I'll do exactly what you want without any objections. Just please let him go and don't hurt him."

Ambrosia seemed to consider her for a long time, but in reality it probably wasn't any longer than twenty seconds. "Okay, but any questions or objections during the mating ceremony, and he will pay. When the ceremony is over, I will let him go, but not until then."

Steph nodded, her throat clogging up, preventing her from saying anything.

"The key."

There was no doubt as to which key Ambrosia was referring, and Steph reached into her bra and handed the woman the key to the prison cells. There would be no more visiting Michael in his cell, not even to say a last goodbye before her mating. The thought had her heart breaking a little more, and the pain in her chest made her suck in a breath.

Ambrosia narrowed her eyes at Michael behind her before an evil smile spread across her face. "True mates. What a waste. You would've made a powerful match, but I already have a deal with Jack, and I've got a feeling he'll be easier to manipulate than this one." She nodded at Michael.

Steph must have looked shocked because the next second Ambrosia gave a short cackle of a laugh.

"You didn't know? What a shame. Go to your room now and make yourself pretty for tomorrow. Jack will expect you to look your best. I'll bring this one back to his cell."

Steph wanted to say something. Beg for a chance to say goodbye to Michael. But doing that might get Michael hurt, and that was out of the question.

She snuck a peek at him as she moved toward the stairs. Just like she had expected, he was under Ambrosia's spell and didn't seem to comprehend what was going on around him. As Steph ascended the stairs, he turned at Ambrosia's command and followed the woman around the corner and down the corridor.

Steph made her way up the stairs and through the house to her room. The pain in her chest had her almost choking, and finally locking the door behind her, she sank down onto the floor. The sobs racking her body had her gasping for breath as the pain in her chest increased even more.

True mates. She had heard it mentioned but discounted as something rare and not worth waiting for. But that was by Jack and his cronies. Based on what Ambrosia had been saying, the bond between true mates was exceptionally strong. But Steph was never going to experience that with Michael. All hope of them being together was lost. Hopefully he hadn't yet realized that they were true mates and never would. That way he could go on to find someone else to mate and be happy.

She had no idea how long she lay on the floor sobbing, but when she finally raised her head, she noticed it was fully dark outside. Her tears had dried a while ago, and a numbness had taken the place of her pain at some stage. It was like someone had removed her heart and filled her chest with cotton wool.

Steph knew what she had to do, and she would do it. The mating would go ahead as planned without any objections from her, but as soon as Michael was set free, she would die. It would reverse Jack's power to its current level as their mating bond died with her, and having already been mated to her, he would never be able to form that kind of bond with anyone else. She would have liked to kill him for what he had done to her, but that would take too much time to plan. Steph had until dawn to plan her own death, and she would make sure it was a watertight plan.

∞∞∞∞

Michael was sitting on the cot in a different cell from the one he had been in earlier. The cuff on his wrist had been replaced with the one mounted to the wall in his new cell.

His mind was a jumble of thoughts. He knew they had been caught somehow, but he couldn't remember what had happened. And there could be only one explanation for that. The witch Ambrosia. He had some vague image in his mind of what she looked like, but he couldn't seem to recall meeting her. In fact, he couldn't remember anything after leaving his cell with Steph. And he was seriously worried about her.

Ambrosia must have caught them right after they walked out of his cell. He wasn't hurt in any way apart from his loss of memory, and he took that to mean the witch was alone when she caught them trying to escape. If Jack had been there, he most likely would have hurt Michael, perhaps repeating what he did at the warehouse. But from what Steph had told him, Ambrosia could force her will on someone and didn't need violence to control a person.

The same reasoning could be used in support of the claim that Steph wasn't hurt either. But more significant was the fact that both Jack and Ambrosia needed Steph in good health for the mating ceremony the next day. The mating bond was important, and the strength of the mating bond was usually dependent on the power of the two people mating. A weak or injured mate would weaken the mating bond, and Ambrosia obviously knew that, having healed Steph once already.

Steph was okay, at least physically, Michael was sure of that. But if she loved him half as much as he did her, she was in pain, and he could do nothing to help her or comfort her. He had already tried everything in order to break or remove the cuff from his arm, but it was designed to hold a shifter like him. There was nothing he could do.

The pain in his chest was severe, like someone was slowly cutting his heart from his body. He knew it wasn't physical pain, but it felt like it. Apparently, the loss of your true mate could kill you. Michael had heard it said, but he had scoffed at the notion. But that was before meeting Steph and realizing that he loved her. There was no doubt anymore that she was his true mate, and he was about to lose her. She would still be alive, but after mating Jack she would be lost to Michael forever.

Something wet landed on his hand, and he felt himself frowning as he looked down. Another drop of wetness landed on his hand as he watched, and he started when he understood what it was. He ran his hand across his face, and it came away wet. Michael stared at it. He couldn't remember the last time he had been crying. It just wasn't something you did as a man or boy in his clowder. Crying was a sign of weakness and was unacceptable even at a young age.

Michael made no effort to stop the tears running down his face. Why should he? He was going to lose the one person he knew he couldn't live without, and it was breaking his heart. There was no life for him after Steph. Without her everything lost its meaning.

But he wouldn't give up hope just yet. It was bleak

but still there until the actual mating had taken place. If he for some reason was let out of his cell before the mating, he would do anything in his power to prevent the mating, even at the cost of his own life. Her life was more important, and her safety would be his focus until all hope was lost.

∞∞∞∞

James studied the grounds of the estate as they drove from the gate toward the main house. It was well maintained and beautiful but still with enough vegetation to easily hide the big cats living there.

They had arrived at the gate ten minutes to two, not wanting to be too early but not too late, either. Duncan, Trevor, and Jennie were in the car ahead of them, and Duncan had made sure they were all let in without any problems. Apparently, the actual mating ceremony wasn't going to start until three o'clock, which gave them some time to look around the place.

"Nice place, but there's no telling how many panthers are hiding in the bushes around here. I don't like it." Carlos was sitting in the passenger seat next to James.

"Yeah, my thoughts exactly." James glanced at his friend. "I think we should stick together while we're here. Particularly since nobody can vouch for us, and we've got no invite to show them if they ask."

"We need to start spreading the word about what's going to happen here today. Since the actual ceremony doesn't start until three, we've got some time. And we might be able to pick up some information about where they're keeping Michael and Stephanie while mingling." The anger in Ann's voice made James's muscles tense like he was preparing to attack. The physical reaction to her emotions was an effect of their strong mating bond.

They parked where indicated by the main house and exited the vehicle. There were people already milling around the grounds, where there were food and drink stations set up for all to enjoy. Most of the guests were already gathered in the area close to the stage, but the actual stage was covered by a tent, hiding the evidence of the barbaric mating Jack was planning.

The three women were soon talking to some of the other females present while James, Carlos, and Trevor were strolling among the guests, listening for any information that could help them in their search for Michael and Stephanie. Duncan had gone off to have a look around inside the house under the pretense of searching for a bathroom. According to Duncan's friend at the gate, the festivities would continue into the evening, giving them some time to search, but the sooner they found Michael and Stephanie the better.

It didn't take long before they started hearing the rumors circulating of the old-fashioned mating practice. They were being spread with accompanying shocked expressions and gasps of horror. James hid a snort of amusement at the effectiveness of their women's rumor mongering. Judging by the guests' reactions to the news, Jack's style of mating wouldn't be well received.

CHAPTER 13

Steph was staring at herself in the mirror. She had just showered and washed her hair. The mating ceremony was supposed to start in just over half an hour, and she was going to meet Ambrosia in Jack's office in a few minutes. Her eyes were swollen and red, and her face was blotchy from all the crying she had done. But that didn't matter to her one bit. What was important was to go along with whatever was asked of her, and Steph would do that. For Michael.

She put on a bra and panties set and the dress she had been given to wear. It was a thin summer dress with a flowery skirt. Nothing fancy at all, and she was actually a bit surprised at that. Jack always wanted to show off, himself as well as what he considered his property. But the dress did nothing to flatter her figure or indicate a high price tag. All it did was cover her flesh and look cheap, which didn't fit with Jack's image at all.

Shrugging, Steph exited her room. She wasn't going

to object to a dress she didn't want. Perhaps most of the attention at the ceremony would be directed at Jack, and that was fine by her. All she wanted was for this to be over as quickly as possible.

She didn't bother to knock before entering Jack's office. As she stepped into the room, she glanced around. Ambrosia was alone in the office, and on seeing Steph, she rose from the couch where she had been sitting.

"Close the door."

Steph did as she was told before approaching the witch.

Ambrosia's lips twisted in disgust as she stared at Steph's face. "I don't want any tears out there."

Steph just nodded. She was ready to take whatever happened to her out there without thinking or reacting. Knowing what she did of what was going to occur, she was already mentally prepared for it. Or at least as much as you could be prepared for being raped in front of a crowd.

Hands came up to cover her eyes, and Steph focused on standing still and not reacting. The tingling didn't take her by surprise this time, and she tried to relax into it and just let it happen.

A couple of minutes later, Ambrosia stepped back and nodded. "You're ready. Stay here, and I'll pick you up and escort you out there in twenty minutes."

Steph nodded, but Ambrosia was already walking away.

∞∞∞∞

Thick manacles on his wrists secured Michael to the

bars of the cage he was in. He had expected them to forget about him until the mating ceremony was over, but instead it seemed he was going to be present at the festivities. To what purpose he had no idea. Perhaps as an example of what would happen to guests who didn't behave. That seemed like something Jack would do.

The two brutes who had come to get him in his cell were the same assholes that had been at the warehouse with Jack. Michael had let them lead him from the cell without giving them any trouble. They exited the house through a back door and then took him to the garage. At first, he had thought they were going to put him in a vehicle, but instead they approached a covered trailer.

It wasn't until he saw what was inside the trailer that he objected. A cage made of thick iron bars was sitting on the trailer bed. It had a cubic shape with a height of about five feet, with manacles in two of the top corners diagonally across from each other.

Michael took the two assholes by surprise when he attacked, and he managed to slam his knee into one guy's crotch. Then a fist caught the side of his face, and before Michael recovered enough to retaliate, he was thrown into the cage. Another shifter joined in, and between the two still standing they managed to secure Michael's wrists in the manacles. They ripped his shirt off his body before closing the cage door and the back door of the trailer.

An engine rumbled to life and the trailer started moving, but it only lasted for a couple of minutes. When the engine was turned off, he could hear a lot of voices outside. It wasn't a stretch to assume that it was the guests present for the ceremony, and that he would be on display for all to see, including Steph.

Steph. Michael was hoping she wouldn't notice him, but the chances of that were slim. If Jack had been informed of their escape attempt, Michael would most likely be used as part of Jack's revenge on Steph. Exactly how, Michael had no idea, but no matter what Jack had planned for him, it wouldn't be pleasant.

∞∞∞∞

"It's time." Ambrosia had opened the door to Jack's office and was beckoning Steph to come with her.

She followed the witch through the house and out through the main entrance. Walking across the parking area in front of the house, she noticed the substantial number of cars parked there and along the drive toward the gate. Judging from the number of cars, there must be at least two hundred people present for the mating, which meant at least a hundred from other panther clans. That was more than she had expected. The clammy fear she had been feeling all day amped up a level.

They approached the back of a platform that had been raised at the edge of an open grassy area. Steph could hear the sound of a multitude of voices like from a large crowd and realized she was at the back of a stage. It was mostly covered by a tent apart from an open corridor to one side rounding toward the front. Following Ambrosia up the makeshift stairs, she felt her heart start to race. This was it. She was walking into her own unwanted mating ceremony, and there was nothing she could do about it.

Her eyes landed on the crowd as she emerged onto the open front of the stage. Steph had been right in assuming that at least two hundred people were present for the ceremony. But she wouldn't be surprised if it was closer to three hundred. They were all staring up at her on the stage with a mixture of fascination and horror on their faces. A strange mix that Steph didn't know what to make of. Most likely it had something to do with her being human. There were plenty of female panthers who resented her since Jack made it known that he had chosen her to be his mate. For some reason they didn't seem to resent him for choosing her, which seemed sexist, to put it mildly.

"Now, here's the lucky woman about to become my mate." Jack grinned and stared at Steph when she swung her gaze to him. "This ceremony will change my life and hopefully all of yours as well."

Steph knew what he was talking about, but she had a feeling few of those people did. The people who didn't know his plans to become their superior would assume he was talking about the usual change that happened to a couple when they mated. And with Jack being a clan alpha, the mating would affect the clan members in some way as well.

"But before that I've got a gift for my soon-to-be mate, as is only befitting the occasion." Jack chuckled and an expression of evil glee spread across his face.

Ice poured into Steph's veins, and her heart stuttered as fear froze her body. Michael. Jack had done something to Michael.

Jack made a sign with his hand and then indicated something at the back of the crowd. Moving her gaze to the place he had indicated, Steph noticed a covered trailer. As she watched, the trailer cover was raised to reveal a cage of thick iron bars, and inside the cage was Michael. Exclamations and gasps came from the crowd. Michael's arms were stretched out to each side and manacled to the cage, revealing his magnificent shirtless upper body. Blood was covering his right cheek and parts of his torso from a cut on his cheekbone, but he had no other visible injuries.

Their eyes met across the distance, and the despair she saw in Michael's gaze almost floored her. Tears started welling up in her eyes, but remembering the consequences her crying would have for Michael's wellbeing, she fisted her hands at her sides and tried to get a handle on her emotions. Her actions weren't going to cause him any more pain than they already had.

Turning away from Michael, Steph stared at Jack with what she hoped was a fairly neutral expression. She had most likely given away her feelings for Michael already, but from this moment onward she would show no more feelings. Nothing to betray her broken heart and her hate for Jack. Her sole focus would be on playing her part in the mating ceremony, and ensuring Michael's safety and freedom by behaving according to Ambrosia and Jack's directions.

***

Michael wanted to scream with grief and rage when he saw Steph enter the stage. There was a crowd of people standing between him and the stage, but he didn't pay any attention to the people gathered there for the ceremony. His only focus was the beautiful woman on stage, and when she met his eyes, the fear and grief he saw there had his whole body tensing with the need to attack the people hurting her.

But he couldn't. There was no doubt he was being displayed before Steph as some form of punishment, and he suspected that anything he said or did would be used as an excuse to hurt and humiliate her. He would like nothing better than to tell the crowd what was going to happen next, but most likely Ambrosia would stop him before he had uttered more than a few words. And then the witch and Jack would take it out on Steph somehow.

Steph broke their eye contact and swung her gaze to Jack. Her whole body stiffened as if she steeled herself for whatever was coming next.

Jack narrowed his eyes as he stared back at Steph. Clearly, he had expected more of a reaction when displaying Michael before her. Then he shrugged and turned his attention to the crowd. "Well, I think it's time, don't you?" Jack waved his hand around, and the tent covering most of the stage was slowly lifted.

Michael felt the blood drain from his face as he took in the setup on stage. The outcries of horror and rage from the crowd reflected his own feelings as nausea rolled through him. His shocked mind was trying to tell him that this must be some elaborate joke. But knowing Jack for the short time he had, Michael knew this was no prank. The alpha panther was even more cruel and evil than Michael had given him credit for.

There was no mistaking the intended use of the frame with its manacles for wrists and ankles. The bar at hip height and the relative placement of the manacles gave Michael a clear impression of how the mating would be carried out. Steph would be bent forward over the bar and secured to the frame giving Jack easy access to force himself into her body.

An agonized scream rose above the noise of the crowd, and it took Michael a couple of seconds to understand that he was the one screaming. His muscles were spasming as his mind was telling him to shift to save his mate, but he fought it. Shifting wouldn't help Steph, and if she had to experience this, the least he could do was to be there for her. Even if he couldn't save her, he would never turn his back on her.

Steph was still standing in the same place when Jack stepped up to her. He grabbed her dress and ripped it from her body. She didn't react, but the hate burning in her eyes was visible for all to see. There was no hiding the fact that she despised Jack and didn't want to mate him.

Michael screamed again, not able to control the rage and grief at witnessing his mate being treated so disrespectfully. His beautiful, strong mate. Silently standing her ground, even though she was about to be raped and unwillingly mated to an evil bastard like Jack.

At the same time the crowd went crazy. People were screaming in outrage at what they were witnessing. Several were trying to get onto the stage, but nobody managed to climb onto the platform. The stage seemed to be protected by an invisible barrier, no doubt another of Ambrosia's powers at work.

"What the fuck is wrong with all of you?" Jack was addressing the crowd with contempt and anger twisting his features. He clearly had complete confidence in Ambrosia's ability to keep him safe from the furious crowd. "Have you never witnessed a proper mating before? Well, you will from now on. This is just the first of many. I'll show you how it's done. But first my mate needs some incentive to show her superior the respect he's due."

Jack stared at Michael across the crowd and gave a sign with his hand. The meaning of the sign soon became apparent to Michael, when his back erupted in pain.

***

The sight of Michael's body twisting in agony had Steph freezing to the spot in shock. This wasn't part of the deal. Ambrosia had promised her Michael wouldn't be hurt, but that had clearly been a lie. A lie Steph had believed without question. Stupid. *I am so fucking stupid.*

The immense ball of fury boiling up inside her made her stagger. Jack laughed, most likely assuming she was about to give up. But that wasn't how she felt. The sound of Jack's laughter just fueled her fury even more, and her whole body started tingling with energy. Like her healing power, only hotter and more potent.

Turning to Jack, she let the power inside her reach out toward him and touch him. The shock on his face as he sank to his knees made her smile, and she released the rest of her power in one large pulse.

Jack was flung backward onto the floor of the stage and slid several meters away from her. His clothes were in tatters and most of his skin was peeling off his body like he had been badly burned. And considering how her power had felt like a ball of fire inside her, it was most likely exactly what had happened. She didn't think he was dead, but she couldn't be bothered checking. Dead or alive he wouldn't be bothering her again, at least not until he was healed. And even then, she doubted it.

Steph glanced around the stage, but Ambrosia was nowhere to be seen. The witch was gone. A shame since she wouldn't have minded hurting the witch as well for what she allowed to happen to Michael.

Michael. Steph turned to look toward the cage he was kept in, not sure what to expect. He was hanging by his manacled arms, clearly no longer able to stand on his knees in the cage. His eyes were filled with agony, but they were staring at her, meeting her gaze. And it was all she needed to see to know that everything would be okay. Any wounds he had she would heal, and he would be all right.

She started moving to jump off the stage but stopped at the sight of the crowd staring at her. Some were slowly backing away from the stage and her, whereas others seemed rooted to the spot. Expressions ranging from awe to horror were on their faces, and she had no trouble understanding why. The show she had just given them had been terrifying, particularly considering hardly anyone knew witches existed. Steph hadn't known herself until the day before, and later she would have to come to terms with being one herself. Because after what she had just done to Jack, there was no doubt as to what she was.

"Stephanie." A female voice rang above the crowd, and Steph's eyes landed on a woman waving at her from the back of the crowd near Michael's cage. Recognizing the woman, Steph jumped down from the stage and ran toward her. It was one of Michael's friends. Some of his male friends were already on the trailer, trying to get into the cage. Steph had no idea how they had been able to find out where Michael was, but she was more than grateful.

She raced to the trailer and climbed up. Staying out of the way of the men trying to open the cage, she reached through the bars and touched Michael's upper arm. "Michael."

Lifting his head, he gave her a weak smile. He was still hanging by his arms, unable to support his own weight on his knees, but he looked at her with love shining through the pain in his eyes. "Steph." Her name was a whisper on his lips.

Leaning to the side to look at his back, she felt tears well up in her eyes. Three deep wounds were running the length of his back, one of them close to his spine. No wonder he couldn't support his own weight. He might not even have any sensation in his lower body.

Her healing power sprang to life, and she started pouring it into him. Closing her eyes, she focused on her power and visualized Michael's wounds knitting together. After a couple of minutes, his body seemed to relax, but she kept going for a few more minutes before opening her eyes and looking at his back. The wounds were closed, and pink scars showed in their place. As she watched, the scars gradually faded and disappeared.

When she turned her head, her eyes stared into smoldering light-brown orbs. The desire in them had her gasping, and she quickly averted her eyes. They were surrounded by his friends, and even though she loved seeing the desire in his eyes, it was still a bit surprising and embarrassing.

"You should put some more clothes on." Michael's

voice was a low rasp.

Steph's gaze snapped to his before looking down at herself. "Oh." She had completely forgotten that she was still only wearing her bra and panties.

Someone cleared his throat beside her. "Here. Take my shirt."

A shirt was handed to her, and she took it before lifting her eyes to the man beside her. "Thank you."

The sound of a snarl from the cage brought her gaze back to Michael. His eyes were narrow with anger as he stared at the man beside her who had just given her his shirt. "Keep your eyes to yourself, wolf."

The man nodded and rose. "You've got it, man."

Steph tried to keep a straight face while focusing on putting on the shirt. Michael's jealousy was like a balm to her soul. With everything she had been through the last few months, seeing the man she loved so clearly irritated that someone else saw her in her underwear, felt amazing to her.

Finally managing to open the cage, one of Michael's friends crept in and started working on the manacles on Michael's wrists. Thankfully, they were easier to open than the locked cage, and as soon as Michael exited the cage, Steph was in his arms. Forgetting the people surrounding them, she pulled him down for a kiss. As his lips captured hers and she opened her mouth to welcome his tongue, all her worries and fears from the last few months drained away. There only Michael and his love for her.

CHAPTER 14

Michael had his arm around Steph as they were sitting close together on one of the couches in Trevor's living room. After picking up a few of Steph's belongings in her room, they had left the estate. Everyone felt a need to talk and discuss what had happened the last few days, and Trevor invited them all to stay at his house in Fearolc to be able to talk freely.

Michael found it hard to sit still. He had found his true mate and almost lost her in the space of a couple of days, and his body was telling him in no uncertain terms to claim her before anything else could happen. The shirt he had borrowed hid his erection, but his pants were tight and uncomfortable.

"I still can't believe how you managed to discover where we were." Steph was smiling gratefully at the people in the room with them. "Without you I don't know if I would've been able to get Michael away from that place." She turned her head and stared up at him with love shining in her eyes.

He just barely kept from kissing her. Giving in to that wasn't a good idea, because he didn't think he would be able to stop there. Kissing would lead to more, and this wasn't the place for that.

"It looked like you were doing pretty well by yourself." Trevor chuckled. "Witches. I always thought they only existed in fairy tales. But of course, I should've known better."

Jennie laughed. She was sitting, wrapped in her mate's arms. Newly mated, they rarely moved out of each other's reach. "You were amazing, Stephanie. Jack had it coming, and forgive me for saying this, but I hope he's dead."

Steph smiled. "Thank you." Then she frowned. "But I don't think Jack's dead. He'll heal and be back to his old self within a few days, unless someone decides to get rid of him. Nobody knows his plans to become the panther king, though, apart from the people in this room and Ambrosia. At least I don't think anyone else knows."

"We'll keep an eye on him." Trevor looked at Duncan, who nodded. "And I think we'll invite the other alpha panthers for a chat. Witnessing what Jack was intending to do on that stage has made an impression. I don't think it will be hard to convince them of Jack's plans to be king. They might decide to take matters into their own hands and put a definite stop to his plans."

"Please tell us if there's anything we can do to help." James was sitting on a couch with Ann, Carlos, and Marna. "And then there's Ambrosia. I don't think we've seen the last of her. If that ritual or spell or whatever it was, was going to increase her power as well as Jack's, she's likely to try again with another alpha."

"And most likely an alpha shifter who's not a panther." Carlos frowned in concern. "A lot of panthers already know who she is. It would be better for her to pick another kind of shifter."

Michael's muscles were starting to cramp, and he changed his position slightly. He agreed with everything being said, but he was struggling to care as much as he should. His cock was throbbing and pushing painfully against the zipper of his jeans. He had a quick shower when they arrived at Trevor's house to wash off the blood on his body, but he hadn't taken the time to do anything about the steel bar between his legs. Getting back to Steph as quickly as possible had been more important to him at the time. At the moment he was regretting his decision not to take care of his raging hard-on while he had the chance.

Steph yawned beside him, and Michael smiled. She had just given him the perfect excuse to get away from the others.

"I hope it's okay if we leave you to it." He looked at Trevor. "Thank you for inviting us to stay, Trevor. I think we'll go rest for a while."

"Of course. Just tell us if there's anything you need." Trevor nodded and smiled, and the rest of the people in the room did as well.

Michael grabbed Steph's hand as they walked out of the room and headed for the bedroom they had been assigned while staying there. It was a large house with plenty of space, and Michael and Steph had been given a room on the first floor. Nobody had said anything or asked any questions about their feelings for each other, and he hadn't volunteered any information, either. They had all seen him and Steph kissing and probably assumed that there was more between them than casual lust, but Michael had done nothing to confirm or deny it. It didn't feel right to say anything about it when he hadn't had a chance to tell Steph that she was his mate. And of course, he had no idea how she would react to him telling her that. Sure, she had wanted to be his mate instead of Jack's, but that was a case of avoiding being mated to someone she hated and not a confirmation of her desire to be Michael's mate. At least that was what he had assumed at the time.

They entered their bedroom, and Michael closed the door behind them. Before he had a chance to say anything, Steph threw her arms around his neck and pulled his head down for a kiss. He really should talk to her before doing anything else, but he couldn't help responding. Her lips were so soft against his, and before he could consciously decide what to do, the kiss heated up. Their tongues tangled and played, and he moaned into her mouth as the taste of her increased his need.

Steph suddenly pulled away and leaned back to stare up into his eyes. Her hand slid up along the hard ridge in his pants, and he moaned again.

"How long have you been like this?" Her eyes were wide, and the desire in them was unmistakable. "Down on the couch you were moving around like you had an itch, but I didn't realize that this was the issue."

She gave his hard shaft a little squeeze as she said the last word, and he sucked in a breath as need spiked through him.

"Steph, please." Michael put his hand over hers and gently removed it from his throbbing cock. "We need to talk."

She frowned and shook her head. "We can talk after I take care of the monster in your pants. I suspect you've been like this for a long time already."

"Steph. I need to tell you something before I make love to you."

"Okay." She sighed. "But I want you to answer my question first."

"More or less since you healed me at the estate."

Gasping she stared at him. "That was hours ago. Are you in pain?"

"It's a bit uncomfortable, but don't worry about that."

Narrowing her eyes at him, she put her hands on her hips. "You should've told me."

"Well, we haven't really been alone since—"

"Even so." Anger was in her eyes as she stared at him, but Michael knew it was because she cared about him.

"Please just hear me out, Steph. Five minutes, okay?"

She sighed again. "Okay, shoot."

It wasn't exactly how Michael wanted to start the conversation, but he needed to tell her. "You're my mate, Steph. I know you probably don't want to—"

"Stop." She was frowning. "I already know we're true mates, Michael, and I've already told you I love you. What is it you think I don't want?"

He was speechless for a few seconds. She knew they were true mates. How did she know that?

Finding his voice again, he stumbled over his words, no doubt looking as shocked as he felt. "You know? I thought… But how? And Jack. It's so soon."

Two hands smoothed up his chest as she leaned against him and stared up into his eyes. The love in her gaze had his heart speed up with hope.

"I love you, Michael. I want to be your mate more than anything in the world. Please make me yours."

Crushing his lips against hers was the only response he had at that moment. He didn't have any words, just actions to show her how much he loved her and wanted her as his mate. She knew they were meant for each other. He didn't know how she knew, and he didn't care. That was something they could talk about later.

Putting his hands on her hips, he slowly slid them up to her sides underneath her T-shirt. Reveling in her soft skin, he reached around her back to unclasp her bra before bringing his hands to her front and cupping her breasts. Steph sighed into his mouth as he gently rolled her nipples between his thumbs and index fingers. His whole body was vibrating with the need to be inside her, but he wanted Steph dripping wet and squirming with desire before he entered her.

Breaking their kiss, Steph stepped back and quickly removed her T-shirt and bra. Michael followed her example by lifting his shirt over his head and discarding it on the floor. Then she was back in his arms, kissing him.

While exploring her mouth with his tongue, he slowly walked her backward until the back of her legs hit the side of the bed. A gentle push and she landed on her back on the mattress with a little shriek. His intentions to go slow were evaporating. Grabbing the waistband of her pants, he quickly pulled them down along with her panties. The scent of her arousal hit him square in the nose, and he realized that his serval was so near the surface his senses were sharper than usual in his human form.

"Your eyes." Steph's voice had his gaze snapping to hers. "They're glowing yellow."

Michael froze. She didn't seem scared, but he didn't want to make the mistake of assuming she wasn't. "Does that scare you?"

She smiled and shook her head. "No, I've seen your animal eyes before, just not this intense."

He smiled back. "So you're okay with it, me, being like this?"

"Oh, Michael. You're gorgeous."

He chuckled. "Gorgeous, huh." Inside, he was strutting with his mate's praise.

Before she could say anything more, he yanked her pants and panties all the way off. After grabbing her legs, he pulled her toward him until her ass was close to the edge of the mattress. He spread her legs and hooked them over his shoulders as he knelt before her. Her pretty pink pussy shone with her juices, and he groaned as his balls pulled up so tightly it felt like they almost lodged in his throat at the sight and scent of her. Using his fingers to spread her folds, he leaned in and sucked her clit into his mouth.

Steph whimpered and tried to close her legs as he sucked and licked her sensitive nub. He really should spend more time warming her up slowly, but he was getting desperate to claim her as his. Using two fingers to breach her entrance, he started moving them slowly in and out of her tight body. Moaning and gripping his hair with both hands, she started rocking her hips against his fingers and mouth.

***

Steph was about to tip over the edge. Pleasure was gathering like heat in her lower belly as Michael's mouth and fingers were attacking all her sensitive parts between her legs. The man knew exactly what to do to drive her crazy. Grinding against him with wanton need, she couldn't help the keening noise she was making. Then his tongue started vibrating, and she rolled over the edge into a cloud of pleasure. He didn't stop, though, but continued his onslaught until he had pulled every ounce of pleasure from her body.

Still panting, she opened her eyes. They landed on Michael standing in front of her. He opened the button on his jeans, and her gaze lowered to his crotch as he pulled down the zipper. He breathed a sigh of what sounded like relief when his thick shaft sprang free.

Steph gasped. His cock was an angry red color, and it seemed to be throbbing. Her channel clenched at the sight of his long, thick member.

"I'm sorry, Steph." His voice was a low rasp. "I don't know how much control I'll be able to maintain. My mind and body have one focus right now, and that is to claim my mate. I won't hurt you, but I don't think I'll be able to go as slow as you deserve, either. If I get too rough, please tell me to stop, okay?"

She shuddered. The thought of Michael fucking her hard was very appealing, to put it mildly. Steph could feel her pussy getting wetter just thinking about it.

"Please, Michael, just fuck me. I want you inside

me." She spread her legs wider in invitation.

Michael's eyes zeroed in on her down there, and his yellow eyes glowed with his need.

She shrieked as he suddenly landed on top of her, catching himself just before he would have crushed her into the mattress. His mouth slanted over hers, and she opened her mouth to his scorching kiss.

After a few seconds, he broke the kiss and pushed up on his hands and knees. "Move." He indicated for her to move to the middle of the large bed.

He followed her and sat back on his knees between her legs. Keeping his eyes on hers, he grasped her ankles and hooked her legs over his shoulders before leaning in and pressing the swollen head of his cock against her entrance. One shallow thrust had the bulbous head breaching her opening, and she moaned at the feeling.

"Look at me."

Steph opened her eyes and met his glowing orbs. She hadn't even realized she had closed them. It just felt so good having him enter her like that.

He slowly moved forward, sliding a bit farther inside her before pulling back a little. A hard thrust had him buried inside her to the hilt, and Steph gasped at the feel of his thick shaft stretching her wide. Snarling, he stared at her as he pulled back and thrust into her again. His thumb found her clit, and he started pumping into her using hard long thrusts while rubbing her sensitive button.

She was panting and whimpering, the powerful sensations of what he was doing to her taking her full attention. Pleasure was building fast in her lower belly, sending her toward the edge at record speed. This man might be the death of her one day. A gloriously pleasurable death caused by orgasmic overload.

Michael groaned, and his pace became erratic. "Come for me, Steph." His voice was strained and rough and almost unrecognizable. Then he growled as he started coming.

Pleasure erupted and barreled through her like a tidal wave, the orgasm growing at the feeling of Michael pumping his seed inside her.

Just as she was starting to come down, Michael bent over her, and a sharp pain stabbed into her shoulder close to the crook of her neck. Opening her mouth, she bit down hard on his shoulder to keep from screaming.

Michael gasped and thrust his cock deep inside her. Another orgasm took her by surprise and flushed the pain away as his hard shaft jumped inside her like a wild thing. It seemed to last forever, with wave after wave of the most powerful pleasure she had ever felt rolling through her. She was gasping for breath by the time she was coming down.

Steph didn't know how long it took before she was able to form coherent thoughts. Opening her eyes, she had to blink a few times before being able to focus.

"You bit me. That was amazing." Michael's voice close to her ear had her turning her head toward him.

She must have heard wrong. He bit her, not the other way around. "You mean you bit me. And, yes, it was amazing. I don't think I've ever come that hard in my life. In fact, I know I haven't."

He grinned, raising his head to look at her. "Yeah, I bit you, but you bit me right back. Fuck, I came so hard I thought my balls were going to explode."

Feeling herself frowning, she studied his face before glancing at his shoulder. She gasped and her eyes snapped back to his. "I'm sorry. I didn't mean to." His shoulder had clear marks from her teeth, blood starting to coagulate in the wounds.

He laughed, then shook his head. "Don't apologize. You marked me. I love it. And I'll heal in no time." Frowning, he looked at her shoulder. "It's worse for you. You take longer to heal. Is it painful?"

Steph could feel a throbbing pain in her shoulder where Michael had marked her, but it wasn't bad. "A little, but not bad."

"Good." He moved his gaze to meet hers. "I don't like it when you're in pain. And I really hate knowing that you will get hurt and not being able to do a damn thing to prevent it. The last couple of days have been hell, and I don't ever want to experience anything like that again."

Her mate. The thought almost brought tears to her eyes. She was no doubt the luckiest woman alive. Putting her arms around his neck, she kissed him. It was intended to be a tender kiss, but as usually happened with Michael, it soon turned heated.

Then he suddenly broke the kiss and moved his head down to her chest. Closing his mouth around one of her nipples, he started licking and sucking on it. She moaned as the sensations caused her clit to start throbbing. Apparently, she was up for another round even after three orgasms.

***

Michael savored the feel and taste of his mate. The urgent need to claim her was gone, and he could finally take his time to worship her like she deserved.

Hands on his chest, pushing him away, made him lift his head and look at her.

Steph grinned. "My turn. I want to have my way with you."

His blood sped to fill his already hardening cock, making it strain with eagerness. "Anything you want, beautiful." Even though his need to claim her was gone, his need for her hadn't diminished.

Steph pushed Michael onto his back, and he was happy to oblige. Straddling his legs, she closed one hand around his cock and started slowly moving it up and down his length. He sighed in pleasure at the feel of her soft hand on him. She bent over him, and he snarled as she sucked him into her wet mouth.

Bobbing her head, she took as much of him as she could into her mouth, her tongue swirling around his sensitive flesh and driving him crazy. One of her hands was working the base of his cock, and the other was fondling his balls, and Michael was quickly racing toward ecstasy. Just as he was about to come, she let go of him and lifted her head to stare at him with a wicked grin.

"You minx." Michael's voice was a low growl as he grinned back at her. "You're going to leave me like this?"

She laughed. "You've done it to me a time or two. But, no, I'm not going to leave you like that. I want you inside me when you come."

She moved up to straddle his hips, and grasping his heavy rod, she guided him to her entrance. Staring into Michael's eyes, she slowly lowered herself onto him, and the sensation of pushing into her tight sheath had him teetering on the edge again in no time. He clamped his jaw shut and focused on not coming.

Steph shuddered when he put his thumb on her clit and started rubbing and lightly pinching the swollen knob between her legs. Focusing on her pleasure helped him hold off, but he wouldn't be able to do it for long.

Panting, she rode him harder and harder until he couldn't keep himself from coming. The orgasm exploded through him, and a couple of seconds later, Steph gasped and her channel clamped down around him. Her orgasm seemed to merge with his own and drive it even higher, and he grabbed her hips and ground into her as her body milked him dry.

Finally coming down, he opened his eyes. "Wow." His voice broke, and he cleared his throat.

"Wow back." Her words were muffled into his chest, having collapsed on top of him after the pleasure took her.

"I've heard that a strong mating bond can bring sex to another level. Now I understand what that means. I thought it was just a sly argument to encourage mating, but it's obviously more than that."

Steph lifted her head and stared down at him. "You mean what just happened has to do with us becoming mates?"

Michael nodded and grinned. "Yeah, which means we can expect it to happen again."

She grinned back at him. "I like the sound of that. It was incredible. I felt your orgasm rush through you, and it triggered my own and added to it. I wouldn't mind doing that again."

"Oh, we will." He raised his head and gave her a quick kiss. "But I think we'll save it for later. Right now, I think we need a shower."

Nodding, she put her head back down on his chest. "Yes, in two minutes."

Michael chuckled and wrapped his arms around his mate. "I love you."

"Love you too."

EPILOGUE

Michael had his arm around Steph. They were standing outside Trevor's large house. Michael's friends had just finished packing their car and were about to return to Edinburgh to continue their vacation there.

James grinned and shook his head. "I didn't think I'd ever see you in love. Mated sure, but in love?" He laughed. "It suits you."

Michael chuckled. "It suits me too." He threw a glance at Steph, who beamed at him. Finally, he understood how newly mated couples felt and why they couldn't keep their hands, and other things, off each other. His mate was his life. Nothing and nobody would ever be more important than her. The only thing that would ever come close was if they had children. And that might happen sooner than he had planned, seeing as they'd completely forgotten about protection since they had mated the day before.

"I guess we'll see you when you decide you've had enough of Scotland then." Carlos had a firm grip on

Marna's hand. Turning to his wife, his eyes dropped to her mouth. "Honeymoon? Maybe we should have another one soon?"

Marna laughed and gave her husband a quick kiss.

Ann snorted and raised an eyebrow in mock irritation. "James, I think we should get these two in the car before we lose even more of our travel companions along the way."

Everyone laughed. Then there was a lot of hugging before James, Carlos, Ann, and Marna got into their car and left, leaving Michael and Steph with Trevor, Jennie, and Duncan.

Michael looked at Jennie. She was standing in front of Trevor, who had his arms wrapped tightly around her. He could see the happiness and love they were both exuding, and it made him smile.

"Jennie and Trevor, I owe you both an apology and a thank you."

They both swung their gazes to him. Jennie shook her head. "No need for that now. It's okay."

"No. I want to apologize for the way I behaved and the pain I caused you both. It was selfish and unacceptable." Michael had already told Steph about how he had tried to get Jennie to become his mate. How he had even gone so far as to lie to his friends, to convince Trevor that Jennie had agreed to become Michael's mate. "And I want to thank you, Jennie, for not letting me push you into something that would've been wrong for both of us."

"Thank you, Michael. I appreciate that." Jennie smiled. "And I'm so happy for you. For you both." She swung her gaze to Steph. "This vacation has been life-changing for all of us I think." Jennie turned her head and smiled lovingly up at Trevor.

The sound of someone walking away had them all turning their heads. Duncan had his back to them as he moved toward the house.

Michael frowned. Duncan was the type of person who seemed to be perpetually amused. At least he had been. But since leaving the panther's estate the day before, Michael couldn't remember seeing the guy smiling even once.

Duncan disappeared into the house and Jennie sighed. "I wonder if something happened yesterday. He seems so down, like he has lost all his joy in life. Have you ever seen him like this before?" Jennie looked up at her mate.

Trevor shook his head, a concerned expression on his face. "No, I'm actually getting a bit worried about him."

∽∽∽∽∽∽

Duncan hurried up to his bedroom and closed the door behind him. A sigh of relief escaped him as he sank down in the chair at the far end of the room, by the large window facing the hills behind the estate. He'd had just about all he could take of happy couples.

His thoughts went for the thousandth time where he didn't want them to go. Sparkling green eyes filled with amusement and desperation looking into his. Framed by long dark lashes designed to bring his gaze to hers and keep it there. Freckles like a sprinkle of cocoa powder covered the pale translucent skin across her straight nose and high cheekbones, making him want to lick her skin to see if she would taste like chocolate. Thick, wild auburn tresses hung past her shoulders. Nothing could have made him look away from her. He had been spellbound.

"Please." She'd repeated the word that had made him turn to look at her in the first place. "Can I please go ahead of you? It's kind of urgent." Squirming, she'd crossed her legs and begged him with her eyes.

Duncan had nodded and taken a step back to allow the wild-haired beauty to move in front of him in the line for the toilets. Words had eluded him. His tongue seemed to be stuck to the roof of his mouth. His usual self would have had a million smart remarks suitable for this situation, but for some reason nothing came to mind.

"Thank you." She'd given him a brilliant smile before moving in front of him. "I hope whoever is in there will hurry up and finish. I'm desperate here." As if to demonstrate how desperate she was, she shoved a hand between her legs and squeezed her thighs together.

Duncan had swallowed as he stared at the woman's sexy round behind, wishing it was his hand shoved between her legs. His cock had twitched, and he'd forced himself to look away from her ass. Berating himself for lusting after a woman desperate to pee, he slowly pulled in a lungful of air to calm himself. Only to be overwhelmed by the sweet aroma of chocolate and something spicy. Perhaps cloves. His cock took notice of her scent and chose that as a perfect excuse to harden up.

"Oh, come on. Please hurry up." Her voice had been low as she muttered to herself in desperation.

As if in answer to her prayer, the door to the only

toilet in the pub swung open, and an older woman stepped out. The beauty in front of Duncan took a couple of steps back to let the older woman pass and collided with his front. Or not quite his front. He had just managed to turn slightly to the side in time to avoid her bumping into him and noticing his rock-hard dick. He was obviously a deviant for getting riled up like that, but he preferred keeping that fact to himself.

The beauty disappeared into the toilet and not three seconds later, a low moan could be heard through the door. The sound had made Duncan grit his teeth as his balls pulled up tight and his cock started throbbing. An image of her bent over in front of him as he pounded into her tight, wet pussy lodged in his brain, and he silently swore.

He wouldn't be able to use the bathroom until his dick softened a bit, and that might take a while judging by the desire wreaking havoc in his body. The best course of action would be to leave and walk off this crazy lust, but he couldn't make himself move away. He needed to see her just one more time before he left.

Duncan stared out of the window as he recalled the scene from two days ago. While the couples had been busy enjoying themselves in their hotel rooms, he had gone to the pub. As the only single person in the group, it had seemed like a good plan. Little did he know that it would bring back old wounds that he had worked hard to bury.

Standing outside the pub toilet, Duncan had tried to come up with something to say to the wild-haired beauty when she emerged. Something smart and funny would be best, and he was still in the process of choosing between a few good options when the door opened.

The woman emerging from the bathroom after relieving herself seemed to be even more breathtaking than she had been just a few minutes earlier. And when she gave him the most stunning smile and thanked him once more for letting her go ahead of him, his mind seized again. He had barely managed to smile back and nod in response. Then she moved past him, and his opportunity to impress her with his wit was lost.

A quick glance over his shoulder had let him know where she was headed. Somewhere to the left of the entrance as far as he could see from where he was standing.

Duncan went into the toilet and locked the door behind himself. His cock was still rock-hard and throbbing. The poor thing probably had a distinct imprint of his jeans' zipper by this time. When he unzipped his jeans, his engorged member sprang free, and he sighed in relief. He couldn't stay in the toilet for long, but it was nice to let the monster out of captivity for a couple of minutes.

Trying to think of mundane things, he'd willed his dick to soften. But nothing happened, and after three minutes, he didn't feel comfortable occupying the toilet any longer. After tucking himself back into his jeans, he had left the toilet and pub, discarding his plans to locate the wild-haired beauty for a chat and perhaps something more.

His mind had been in turmoil as he walked back to the hotel. Constantly tossing arguments back and forth about the feasibility of going back to the woman at the pub. But his massive erection was a sound argument against returning. His shirt hid the thick ridge in his pants from view, but if his shaft didn't soften soon, it would start to get painful. And considering how little it took to rile him up, talking to the beautiful woman who'd caused it would only make it worse.

Arriving in his hotel room, he'd quickly discarded his clothes in a pile on the floor and gone into the shower. He wrapped a hand tightly around his straining member, and his whole body jerked at the powerful sensation. His cock seemed to be extra sensitive for some reason, and he had to clamp his mouth shut to avoid making too much noise as he moved his hand quickly up and down his swollen member. Images of the beauty at the pub assailed him, and before he could brace himself, his knees buckled as a tidal wave of pleasure rolled through him. Ecstasy continued to pound through his body as he emptied his balls in powerful bursts, until he was left breathing heavily, kneeling under the spray of the shower.

"Fuck me," Duncan had muttered to himself. Jerking off was something he did often being a healthy single shifter, but his orgasms weren't usually that all-consuming and powerful, and they didn't usually leave him quite so spent. He had a feeling it had something to do with the beautiful woman who had set his body on fire with need from just smiling at him. And of course, her amazing scent. His mouth watered at the thought.

The landscape outside his bedroom window started registering as Duncan came back from reliving the events from two days ago. Again. If he didn't know better, he would have seriously considered the possibility that the wild-haired beauty was his mate. But that was impossible.

"Fuck." He swore a second time, but for a completely different reason. All the old pain and resentment rose up and threatened to consume him. For so long he had managed to keep those feelings locked down tightly and lived his life like he didn't have a care in the world. But at the moment he was powerless to prevent everything from surfacing again. Duncan had already met his mate years ago, and she had rejected him.

He urgently needed something else to focus on to avoid being swallowed by the pain of losing his mate. Or rather someone. And he knew the perfect candidate.

---THE END---

BOOKS BY CAROLINE S. HILLIARD

Highland Shifters

A Wolf's Unlikely Mate, Book 1
Taken by the Cat, Book 2
Wolf Mate Surprise, Book 3
Seduced by the Monster, Book 4
Tempted by the Wolf, Book 5
Pursued by the Panther, Book 6
True to the Wolf, Book 7 – May 2023
Book 8 – TBA

Troll Guardians

Captured by the Troll, Book 1
Saving the Troll, Book 2
Book 3 – TBA

ABOUT THE AUTHOR

Thank you for reading my book. I hope the story gave you a nice little break from normality.

I have always loved reading and immersing myself in different worlds. Recently I have discovered that I also love writing. Stories have been playing in my head for as long as I can remember, and now I'm taking the time to develop some of these stories and write them down. Spending time in a world of my own creation has been a surprising enjoyment, and I hope to spend as much time as possible writing in the years to come.

I'm an independent author, meaning that I can write what I want and when I want. I primarily write for myself, but hopefully my stories can brighten someone else's day as well. The characters I develop tend to take on a life of their own and push the story in the direction they want, which means that the stories do not follow a set structure or specific literary style. However, I'm a huge fan of happily ever after, so that is a guarantee.

I'm married and the mother of two teenagers. Life is busy with a fulltime job in addition to family life. Writing is something I enjoy in my spare time.

You can find me here:
caroline.s.hilliard@gmail.com
www.carolineshilliard.com
www.facebook.com/Author.CarolineS.Hilliard/
www.amazon.com/author/carolineshilliard/
www.goodreads.com/author/show/22044909.Caroline_S_
Hilliard

CAROLINE S. HILLIARD

Printed in Great Britain
by Amazon